MURDER IN THE DARK

By Betsy Reavley

First published in 2018 by Bloodhound Books

www.bloodhoundbooks.com

Print ISBN: 978-1-9129 86-03-3

Also by Betsy Reavley

Beneath The Watery Moon
Carrion
The Quiet Ones
The Optician's Wife
Frailty
Pressure
Murder At The Book Club

Praise For Betsy Reavley

"A deliciously Agatha Christie-style mystery that sucks you in from the first page." **Sibel Hodge bestselling author of Look Behind You**

"A good old Whodunnit from Ms Reavley that will keep readers guessing till the very end!" **J.A. Baker Bestselling author of The Other Mother**

"A deliciously devilish whodunit!" **Robert Bryndza bestselling author of the Detective Erika Foster Series**

"Holy freaking hell Betsy is back with a new psychological thriller and she is on fire!" **Shell Baker – Chelle's Book Reviews**

"The plotting is excellent and the pacing spot-on. A deep sense of foreboding and growing peril permeates the entire novel." **Mark Wilson – Author**

"PRESSURE by Betsy Reavley is a unique and utterly compelling thriller that will suck you in from the very beginning and drag you down into its murky depths along with its characters." **Linda Green – Books Of All Kinds**

"A captivating, chilling, at times gruesome thriller by our own lady of suspense: Betsy Reavley!" **Caroline Vincent – Bits About Books**

"A super-fast paced thriller that I felt I had to read just as fast, as if my own reading-oxygen was in short supply." **Michelle Ryles – The Book Magnet**

"This book is such a creepy thrill ride, I was just blown away from the very beginning." **Ashley Gillan – (e)Book Nerd Reviews**

"Intense, toe curling, action packed, spine tingling, and absolutely brilliant." **Kaisha Holloway – The Writing Garnet**

"The pacing of the story is really good especially if you prefer a character driven story with twists strategically placed to really catch you out." **Rachel Broughton – Rae Reads**."

"Bursting with suspense and intrigue, Pressure is an atmospheric thriller that'll keep you glued to the pages and guessing right to the end." **Aileen Mckenzie – Feminisia Libros Reviews**

"Pressure is the ultimate locked room mystery and I advise you put a few hours aside and read this in one seating just don't forget to breathe!!" **Ellen Devenport – Bibliophile Book Club**

"Pressure is a fast paced thriller which is genuinely terrifying." **Joanne Robertson – My Chestnut Reading Tree**

"Betsy Reavley has gone and smashed it with her newest book Pressure, pure unadulterated tension which will intensify the fire within your imagination." **Diane Hogg – Sweet Little Book Blog**

"This is a great, fast paced and claustrophobic story that will keep you on the edge of your seat." **Jessica Bronder – JBronder Book Reviews**

"An addictive, compelling read that pushed me well out of my comfort zone - if you like disturbingly twisty plot lines and dark characters then this is definitely the read for you." **Lisa Hall, Author of the best selling psychological thriller Between You and Me**

"The Optician's Wife is a stylish, brilliantly crafted thriller which really delivers. A very real sense of creeping dread, combined with intelligent, finely drawn characters, had me turning the pages late into the night. This one will linger with you, long after the book is finished. Reavley has delivered a masterclass and deserves to be up there with the best in the business." **L J Ross – Bestselling author of The DCI Ryan books.**

"I love discovering new authors especially one who can shock and surprise me like this as it doesn't happen very often!" **Joanne Robertson – My Chestnut Reading Tree**

"Don't you just love it when you pick up a book and it blows you away, well Betsy Reavley has managed to do just that with a book that's absolutely filled with suspense and intrigue." **Lorraine Rugman – The Book Review Cafe**

"This was a fantastic book and one I knew from the first chapter it was going to keep me enthralled reading it." **Leona – Goodreads Reviewer**

"Wow! What a stunning book. Draws you in, spins you a line and boom! you've got it completely wrong. Loved it. So clever." **MetLineReader – Goodreads Reviewer**

"This is a book that once you start reading it you won't be able to stop. It is a story that grabs you right from the very beginning." **Joseph Calleja, Relax and Read book Reviews**

"This is true stand-out in the domestic noir genre." **Caroline Matson, Confessions of a Reading Addict**

"I've learned that people will forget what you said,
people will forget
what you did, but people will never forget
how you made them feel."
Maya Angelou

"Bad people are to be found everywhere, but even among the worst
there may be something good."
Dostoyevsky's The House of the Dead

Minstrel Man
By Langston Hughes

Because my mouth
Is wide with laughter
And my throat
Is deep with song,
You did not think
I suffer after
I've held my pain
So long.
Because my mouth
Is wide with laughter
You do not hear
My inner cry:
Because my feet
Are gay with dancing
You do not know
I die.

For my children.
Reach for the stars.

Prologue

1.34am Friday 13th December

The cold winter sunlight streamed in through the glass window, highlighting the polish on the brown leather shoes that were dangling in the air. Outside, the world was just going to sleep and the doors of Ashton's Bookshop would remain closed until Matilda Edgely arrived to open them.

But while Matilda was at home, sleeping peacefully in her bed, she was blissfully unaware of the discovery she would make later that morning. Because inside Ashton's, hanging from a rope that was attached to the rafters at the back of the shop, was the body of the shop owner, Dennis Wade.

And from a leather, high-back armchair the killer looked up at the victim, smiling.

Chapter 1

Matilda Edgely was doing her best to iron the creases out of her blue shirt, while keeping half an eye on the toaster, hoping that her breakfast wouldn't burn. The cheap plastic clock on the wall of her basement flat ticked loudly, reminding her not to be late for work.

Matilda, or Tilly as her friends knew her, had worked at Ashton's Bookshop for six months. As a university student at Jesus College in Cambridge, she was working part-time to fund her education.

Since she was very young, Tilly had known she wanted to become a vet and had worked extremely hard at school to achieve the results she needed to make it all the way from Devon to Cambridge University. Her parents, who were proud as punch, helped as best they could but were not in a financial situation to do very much. Tilly, who loved her mum and dad, was more than happy to knuckle down and do what needed to be done by herself. She had always been independent. Being born without a silver spoon in her mouth had taught her how to stand on her own two feet and fight for what she wanted.

Frustrated that despite her best efforts the creases were not coming out of her cotton shirt, Tilly unplugged the iron and sat down to eat her Marmite on toast, while watching the breakfast news show. That December morning felt no different to any other. The only noticeable thing was the light covering of snow on the ground outside. Tilly groaned when she realised it would be better to walk to work than cycle, like she normally did, on her trusty old red Raleigh.

Still in her dressing gown, Tilly picked up the still wrinkled shirt and took it into her small bedroom to get dressed. She shared the flat with one other student; a Chinese woman who was studying economics. They were friends but, in truth, Tilly found Yuki slightly irritating. Especially when she cooked Cantonese food that made the whole flat smell of shrimp paste. Yuki was also not so good at keeping the kitchen clean, and Tilly often found herself trying to scrub soy sauce marks off the kitchen surface.

After dressing, Tilly tidied away her breakfast things before reaching for her coat, bobble hat and gloves. It looked cold outside and the walk from her flat on Maids Causeway to the bookshop on Trinity Street would take her fifteen minutes.

She presumed Yuki was still asleep, since her door was shut, so Tilly closed the front door softly behind her. Then she set off to work, her breath leaving cloud trails as she walked briskly along the icy pavement, being careful not to slip.

On that Friday morning, Cambridge was quiet. A number of schools had closed because of the snow. The weatherman had warned of more to come. It would be all most people could talk about. The British loved discussing the weather.

Putting her headphones in, Tilly made her way along King Street towards the Market Square and listened to Florence and the Machine. She'd seen them play at Glastonbury once and had been an avid fan ever since.

Sinking her gloved hands into the pockets of her duffle coat, she felt the keys with her fingers knowing that at the same time next week, she would be at home in Devon with her parents, preparing to celebrate Christmas.

Although she liked Cambridge very much, it was a world away from Ilfracombe, the seaside town her family now lived in. She missed being by the sea and loved returning home. Tilly told herself that once she had become a vet, she would return to that part of the world and start a small practice of her own. It was the dream she'd had since she was eight years old and it had not lost its appeal over the last seventeen years.

As she turned onto Trinity Street, she stopped for a moment to look at the wintery scene. Large flakes were falling from the sky and the university buildings on her left looked glorious in the snow. It was as if time had stood still. Tilly could imagine students throughout the ages walking those same cobbled stones, on their way to classes. The thought filled her with warmth. She liked the idea of a simpler era, before smart phones and the Internet. It was one of the reasons she loved Ilfracombe so much: it was untouched by time.

Snapping out of her daydream Tilly hurried along the street to the shop, not wanting to be ticked off by her boss for being late. Although it was her job to open up the shop, she never arrived before Dennis, who was always sitting behind the counter when she got there, even if she was early.

But as she approached the door, she realised something felt different. Inside, the lights were off and as she went to open the door, she discovered it was already unlocked. The room was dark, and Tilly called out, 'Dennis? Are you there? Sorry if I'm a few minutes late.'

She turned on the light switch and saw the body of her employer hanging from a rope. But Tilly didn't scream. She turned the lights off and turned and walked out of the shop. With a shaking hand, she pulled off one of her gloves, removed her phone from her bag, called 999, and asked to be put through to the police.

'Police, what's your emergency?'

Tilly froze suddenly, unable to talk. What should she say?

'Hello?' The responder asked down the phone.

'I…' But the words wouldn't come.

'Miss?'

'Trinity Street.' She managed finally. 'Ashton's Bookshop. Come quick.' It was all she could say before she felt her legs go from under her and she found herself sitting on the pavement in the snow.

Staring down at the phone she held in her hands, Tilly suddenly wondered if she was having some sort of episode and had imagined the whole thing. Had she? Was Dennis really inside? But she knew it wasn't her imagination, and that what she had seen was very real, and the moment she let herself accept it tears began to stream down her cheeks.

It had never occurred to her to ask for an ambulance. It was as clear as day that Dennis Wade was dead. No living human had that skin colour.

She'd never seen the body of a dead person before. Her experience was limited to the corpses of animals as part of her course.

Still unable to stand, Tilly sat crying in the snow while the cold wetness soaked through her black trousers. Her whole body began to shake as the shock set in. Her mind was whirling, trying to process what she'd just seen. Her boss was dead. Her boss had killed himself. Her boss had left her to find his body.

In the distance, she could hear the sound of sirens approaching and although she hoped it would help her to feel better, the noise only represented dread.

Trinity Street, which was normally a pedestrian zone, soon emptied as the police car came screeching down the narrow street. Early morning shoppers dashed out of its path, stopping to watch the drama unfold.

The Mercedes hatchback stopped right in front of Ashton's and two uniformed officers got out, both wearing high-vis jackets. The female officer, who was noticeably short, approached Tilly and bent down on her heels.

'Are you the woman who called it in?' she asked, her Peterborough accent recognisable to Tilly.

'Yes,' Tilly answered in a daze.

'In there?' The officer pointed. Tilly nodded. 'Help her up…' The female officer turned to her male colleague. 'She'll catch her death.'

The male officer, who was younger than his female counterpart, did as he was told and guided Tilly to the car, where he helped her into the back seat and got out a foil blanket.

Tilly watched as the woman removed a small torch from her belt and slowly opened the shop door.

Minutes later she reappeared looking pale and shook her head solemnly before reaching for her radio. 'Deceased male at Ashton's Bookshop. We need forensics and this building needs to be cordoned off,' she spoke into the radio.

The male officer stood leaning against the car with his arms folded trying to retain some warmth.

'Suicide is it?' the male officer asked.

'Don't think so.'

'Huh?'

'Well, he's strung up high and there's no sign of how he got up there,' the female said seriously. 'Has she said anything?' She signalled to Tilly.

'Not a word. The girl's in shock.'

'An ambulance is on the way.' The officer turned to look at the shop. 'We need to keep the public away,' she added, referring to the crowd of onlookers who had gathered nearby. 'Bloody nosy parkers.'

The male officer, who had a neatly trimmed beard, went and stood in the bookshop doorway and again folded his arms. No one was getting past him unless he said so.

Tilly sat in the back of the car watching it all unfold. All she could think about was Dennis Wade's wife. She'd never met the woman, but she'd often heard Dennis speaking fondly of her. Tilly was sure they had children too. The thought made her stomach churn.

As the passenger door opened, Tilly looked up to see the kind face of the officer.

'Can you tell me how you know the deceased?'

'I work in the shop. He is…' Tilly paused, '…was, my boss.'

'I see.' The officer smiled sadly. 'What's your name?'

'I'm Matilda Edgely. I was meant to open up but he was always here before me. He loved the shop.' Tilly swallowed hard.

'I need you to give me his name and address, please.' She removed a small note pad from her luminous jacket pocket.

'Dennis Wade. He lives in Barton with his wife.' Tears pricked her eyes. 'I don't know the address.'

'That's very useful information. Thank you.' She closed the car door and returned to jotting on her notepad.

Watching passers-by looking at her sitting in the back of the police car, Tilly began to feel like a criminal. She sunk down into her seat and wished she were back in bed. The day had not started the way she had intended.

Chapter 2

Twenty-five minutes later, DCI Barrett and DI Palmer were at the scene. Barrett, who seemed strangely unaffected by the bitter cold, pulled on a pair of shoe protectors, while Palmer tried to hide his face in his tightly wound scarf.

'Hello, sir,' the short officer welcomed her boss.

'What do we have here?' Barrett said, stepping into the bookshop.

'Dennis Wade. He is the owner. Matilda Edgely, who works here, discovered the body this morning.'

'Right.' Barrett stood looking up at the stiff body that hung from one of the old beams in the ceiling.

'Who else has been in here?' he asked, walking around in a circle to get a look at the body from all sides.

'Only me, sir.' The officer did everything she could to avoid looking at the corpse.

'Good. Keep it that way.' Barrett stopped and bent down to inspect the floor.

'What is it, sir?' Palmer asked, pulling the scarf down from over his mouth and nose.

'Marks, look here.' Barrett removed a pen from his grey suit jacket and pointed at the scuffs and a puddle on the ground. 'Make sure SOCO get a picture of this,' Barrett barked, standing upright and returning the pen to his inside pocket.

'Yes, sir,' the officer responded.

'How did he get up there?' Palmer asked, following the rope from its position around Wade's neck, up to the rafters and then down the staircase on the left side of the room where it was tied.

'Who put him up there, you mean,' Barrett corrected his colleague. 'Very good question.' His face was the same shade of grey as his suit. 'As soon as we have an address for the victim we'll pay a visit to his wife.' Barrett turned to Palmer who nodded gravely.

'I'll go and speak to the girl who found him.' Palmer was keen to get away from the crime scene and the lifeless, hanging body.

The skin around the dead man's neck was raw and the thick rope cut into it. Palmer could also see that the corpse had soiled himself. The scent of ammonia in the air was unmissable, as was the puddle on the floor beneath the body.

'That's no way to go,' Palmer shook his head, muttering under his breath as he left the shop on his way to interview the woman who had made the discovery.

When Palmer opened the rear door on the passenger side of the car, he was surprised by the age of the woman he found. He'd been expecting someone older, someone dusty-looking, but Matilda Edgely was young and, under other circumstances, could be called attractive. Palmer had to admit he didn't spend much time in bookshops but, if he had, he would have not been expecting to be served by her. The name Matilda he associated with an older woman.

'DI Palmer. You're Matilda, I gather?' He bent down on his haunches and introduced himself to the frightened looking woman.

'I can't believe it.' Her eyes were wide, and she appeared like a deer in the headlights.

Poor kid, Palmer found himself thinking, despite the fact he was only fifteen years her senior.

'Can you tell me a bit about Mr Wade? I know it's been a shock.' Looking down at his feet he realised he was still wearing his shoe protectors in the snow. If it wasn't such a serious situation, he might have chuckled.

'He was a nice man. I didn't spend time with him away from the shop, so I can't tell you much, but he was always respectful.

Never lost his temper or anything. People who came into the shop liked him. He made an effort to help local authors, and arranged meet-ups and signings. I can't imagine why he would do this.'

That's the difference between an officer and a citizen, Palmer told himself, *the ability to spot when a crime had taken place.*

'What about his home life, Matilda?' Palmer asked removing the shoe protectors. Her name did not sit easily on his tongue.

'I don't know much about that. Like I said, we worked together but that was it.'

'How many other people work in the shop?' Palmer stood up and rubbed his hands together in an attempt to escape the cold.

'There are usually four of five of us at one time. It's a large place.' Her eyes darted over, and she stared helplessly at the front window.

'Could you possibly give me a list of all the names of other employees?' He reached into his coat pocket and removed a notepad.

'Yes, of course.' Matilda's brow furrowed. 'Well, there is Jane Campbell. She's also my manager and she sometimes works on the till. And Aiden Gerrard: he works in the stock room. Myleene Little: she's on the till upstairs, usually. And then Amber Wu: she's part-time.' Tilly paused, searching her memory for any more information that might help. But the shock had taken its toll on her.

'It's okay,' Palmer soothed. 'Take your time.'

Tilly closed her eyes and a large teardrop ran down her pale cheek.

'Marcus Goldman. He does the accounts.' Her eyes opened, and Palmer thought he saw something akin to fear cross her face for a moment. 'And Steven Fisher, he works part-time, too.'

'You've been very helpful, Matilda.' Palmer finished scribbling the names down in his pad.

'Matilda was my grandmother's name. People usually call me Tilly.'

'I see.' It now made sense to Palmer. 'Is there someone you'd like me to call for you?'

Tilly paused a moment and considered this. 'No, there is no one.'

Fifteen minutes later, Barrett was informed that officers back at the station had tracked down an address for the deceased.

'Come on, Joe,' Barrett barked as he marched out of the shop. 'You're coming with me.'

Palmer jumped to attention and went scampering after his boss; a man who never minced his words and often forgot about common courtesy.

'You drive, we're going to Balsham.' Barrett flung the keys at his partner as the snow began to fall more heavily. 'I hate driving in this weather.'

As they got into the car Palmer immediately started the engine before fiddling with the heater, much to Barrett's disapproval. He was keen to talk to Dennis Wade's wife as soon as possible but, as they made their way through the congested town centre, it became apparent that the weather had other ideas.

Large light flakes fell in a flurry, making it difficult to see too far ahead, despite the frantic work of the windscreen wipers.

Balsham is a small village to the south east of the city. The roads outside of the city had not been salted and made for hazardous driving conditions. Palmer, who was a careful man, refused to go at the speed Barrett would have liked, but as the car wheels slid when he took a turning into the village Barrett quickly stopped looking so impatient. And, with Balsham being a small village, it didn't take them long to find number 2 May's Avenue, which was just off the high street.

Barrett eyed the house as he got out of the car, surprised to see there were no lights on.

Number 2 May's Avenue was a 1960s house, built with yellow-orange brick. It had a neat front garden and there was a garage to the left of the semi-detached cottage.

Barrett didn't wait for Palmer and was by the front door before his partner had managed to lock the car. The pavement was icy, and Palmer was careful as he manoeuvred his way along the concrete slabs.

They rang the doorbell twice and knocked loudly, but the house did not spring into life and Barrett feared no one was home. 'Shit,' he muttered stepping back from the door so that he could get a better look at the house.

'No one there, sir,' Palmer commented, stating the obvious as he noticed a cat jump onto the windowsill inside the house. 'Well, maybe not no one.' He grinned pointing at the cat. Barrett shot him an icy stare. This was no time for joking about, and just as Barrett was about to say exactly that, he saw the next-door neighbour peer out from behind their net curtain.

'Someone has to be feeding it.' Barrett cocked his head in the direction of the cat before approaching the door of number 4, followed closely by Palmer.

A woman, who was in her seventies, tentatively opened the door and peered out. 'What you want?' she asked suspiciously.

'I'm DCI Barrett of Parkside Police Station. We are looking for a Mrs Veronica Wade. Do you know where she is?'

Clearly surprised to discover the police on her front doorstep asking about Veronica, the elderly lady opened the door wider, to reveal she was still in her night dress and dressing gown.

'Veronica… she's gone to stay with her sister. Why do you want to know?' She had no fear asking questions.

'It is a private matter. Do you have a contact number or an address?' Palmer had come across old biddies like this before and he knew how to deal with them.

'Her sister lives in Somerset, I think. What's happened?' Her little blue eyes fixed Palmer's.

'Do you know where in Somerset, perhaps?'

'I think near Cheddar. Somewhere like that.' She tucked her gnarled hands into her off-white dressing gown.

'Do you have a name for Mrs Wade's sister by any chance?' Barrett asked, growing impatient again.

'Francesca, I think, but don't know if she's married or what not.' The elderly lady ran a hand over her unkempt bed head in an attempt to smooth it.

'Can I take your name, please?' Palmer offered his most charming smile.

'Peggy Wilkinson.' Her voice remained gruff, but Palmer could tell she was thawing.

'When was the last time you saw Mr Wade?' Barrett asked.

'Oh, it was yesterday morning. He's very good to me. He helps me put my bins out and it was bin collection day, so he came and knocked.'

'Did you talk about anything in particular?' Barrett pressed.

'The weather mostly. Just chitchat. Why are you asking me about Dennis?'

'Thank you so much for your time.' Palmer beamed another smile at her and both men excused themselves, leaving her standing in the doorway, letting in all the cold as she watched them go out of sight.

'We should have asked her if she has a key for the house. Someone will need to take care of that cat,' Palmer said looking back at the feline, which was meowing from inside.

'Let's track down the sister first, then let's worry about the bloody moggy.' Barrett got back into the passenger seat and removed his mobile phone.

'Where to next, sir?' Palmer asked starting the ignition and looking forward to the blast of warm air that would soon be blowing in his face.

'Back to the scene. The SOCOs should be there now and I'd like to watch them work. We'll leave them to sort out tracking down the sister at HQ.'

'Convenient perhaps, that Mrs Wade is away,' Palmer mused.

'Perhaps.' Barrett stared out the window watching the rows of white fields going by. Unlike many, he loved the wintertime – partly because he had a tendency to sweat whenever the sun was out and partly because the summer reminded him of happier times with his wife, before she lost her battle with breast cancer, five years earlier.

'They say this weather is going to last for a few weeks. I hope not,' Palmer groaned.

'The cold suits me, Joe. I like it.'

'Glad someone does, sir,' Palmer scoffed.

'Let's hope we get this case wrapped up quickly.' Barrett changed the subject. 'Otherwise we will all be working over Christmas.'

Palmer nodded in agreement. He couldn't bear the idea of letting down his son and wife again. The job sometimes had to come first but it pained him to miss out on quality time with them both, especially at a time like this. Palmer made a promise to himself that he would work even harder than usual to get the case solved so that he could then, hopefully, enjoy a few days off with his family.

By the time Barrett and Palmer had returned to the crime scene it was awash with press, police and scene of crime officers. As before, tourists enjoying Cambridge in the snow had stopped to see what was happening.

'We need to get that CCTV checked,' Palmer said pointing up at a small camera that was attached to a lamppost, close to the entrance of the shop.

'Yes. Good.' Barrett wandered off in the direction of the bookshop waving at one of the SOCOs as he went.

'Good to see you, Bob,' Barrett said, shaking hands with a man dressed head-to-toe in white.

'Got yourself another murder.' Bob was pulling on blue nitrile gloves as he spoke.

'Bit of a grizzly one,' Barrett told his colleague.

'The grizzlier the better.' Bob winked as he headed indoors and out of the bitter cold that was blowing around the narrow, cobbled street.

Barrett liked Bob and his enthusiasm for the job, but he could never understand the man's attitude. Barrett wondered if Bob joked in order to make the work easier and hoped that was the reason.

'Not a suicide then,' Bob chimed before he'd barely entered the room. He was an expert in his field and could read a crime scene in moments.

'Doesn't look like it,' Barrett agreed, standing back to let his fellow officer work the scene.

'Our perpetrator has made no attempt to conceal the murder. This was personal.' Bob strained to get a better look at the man hanging from the ceiling.

'Been reading those profiling books again.' Barrett rolled his eyes. He was a copper who believed in good old-fashioned policing.

'Just saying what I see.' Bob continued to walk methodically around the room.

'The finger.' Bob pointed at Dennis Wade's right hand. 'You see that?'

The room was still dark, and fellow officers erected lights. They couldn't turn on the light switch until it had been dusted for prints.

As Barrett squinted, he saw what Bob was referring to. Dennis Wade's little finger was missing.

Chapter 3

1.43pm Friday 13th December

Tilly was driven home from the police station. They had brought her there to take her prints so, they told her, that she could be eliminated from their investigation. Not wanting to appear guilty of anything, Tilly had agreed.

When she returned to her basement flat she was relieved to find Yuki, her flatmate, sitting on the sofa and talking fast in Chinese on the phone.

Yuki's perfectly plucked eyebrows rose when a police officer escorted Tilly inside.

'The DCI will probably want to ask you more questions, miss.' The officer stood tall in his high-vis coat.

'That's fine.' Tilly sank into the sofa next to Yuki and started to rub her temples. 'Thank you.'

The officer nodded before letting himself out.

'What you do?' Yuki had hung up the phone and turned her full attention to Tilly. She was wearing a grey fluffy onesie, which swamped her small figure.

'Mr Wade, the bookshop owner, I found him this morning dead in the shop.' She memory of the image made her well up again. 'He killed himself.'

'You what?!' Yuki put her slender arm around her friend. 'Poor Tilly. Awful. Why you not call me?'

'I didn't know if you were awake. You were sleeping when I left.' The excuse sounded feeble, but it was the only one she had.

'I so sorry Tilly. I would come.' Her poker-straight black hair shimmered like satin in the low winter light that forced its way through the grubby window.

'I know.' She sniffed. 'I need a drink.' Tilly looked down at her shaking hands.

'I get whisky from shop.' Yuki sprung up out of her seat and darted for the door.

'No, no need. There is some vodka in the cupboard. That will do.'

'No.' Yuki was insistent. 'Whisky good for shock.'

Tilly smiled at her petite flatmate, suddenly very grateful for her company.

'The vodka will be fine.'

Yuki, realising that she'd lost this time, shrugged and returned to the sofa.

'I never seen dead person.' Her grasp of the English language left a lot to be desired.

'No, me neither,' Tilly said reaching for a glass and pouring herself a healthy measure of vodka. 'You want one?' She held the bottle up to Yuki, who giggled behind her hand at the thought.

'No. Too early for me.' Yuki held her hands up.

'Well normally it would be too early for me too…' Tilly glugged the cold vodka and then wrinkled her nose. 'Do you have anything on today?'

'Cooking. Friends come for food later.' It was the answer Tilly had been dreading.

'I teach you Chinese cooking?' Yuki was doing her best to be a friend.

'Do you know what…' Tilly smiled. 'That would be great.'

'You no have job now. Maybe you be chef.'

'Not sure it's quite my thing.' Tilly paused. It hadn't dawned on her that her job was in jeopardy but, of course, there was no way that the shop would open again any time soon. She gave a small shudder. 'So what are we cooking then?'

'I show you how make dumpling.'

'Pork?'

'No pork. Lamb.' Yuki went over to the fridge and removed a white plastic bag full of raw meat.

The sight of it instantly reminded Tilly of the dead body that she had seen hanging only two hours earlier. Dennis Wade had looked like an animal carcass in an abattoir. Putting her hand over her mouth to stop the vomit spilling onto the floor, she dashed towards the bathroom leaving Yuki standing in the kitchen looking confused.

When Tilly returned, five minutes later, she looked worse than she had when she'd entered the flat, escorted by the policeman.

'You sick?' Yuki stood holding a knife.

'Just the vodka.' Tilly swallowed down another wave of sickness, the taste of bile still fresh in her mouth. 'I think I'm going to go and lie down.'

'Okay. I save you dumpling.' Yuki returned to chopping up Chinese leaves.

'Thanks,' Tilly said, her throat raw from vomiting, as she went into her bedroom and closed the door.

It was cold in their basement apartment, so Tilly got into bed, fully clothed, and pulled the covers up around her face. She needed the job at Ashton's Bookshop so she could afford to study. The realisation that this was now being threatened left her miserable.

For the first time since discovering the body, she realised what she needed to do was call home and hear the sound of her mum's voice. Reaching out from beneath the warmth of the duvet she picked up her mobile phone and dialled her parents' number.

'Hello?' The soothing tone of her father's voice echoed down the line.

'Dad, it's me.' Tilly felt the tears welling up again.

'How are you, my love?'

'I've had a bit of a rough morning.' She didn't want to frighten him.

'What's up, kid?'

'Well, my manager, I went to work this morning and I found him dead.'

There was a pause on the phone while her father absorbed the unexpected information and Tilly found herself biting her nails, something she hadn't done since she was young.

'You poor child. How awful. What happened?'

Tilly proceeded to explain and her father listened silently, occasionally letting out a small gasp.

'You should come home. You should not be in the city dealing with this by yourself.' Her father had always lived in villages his entire life and never really entertained the idea of city living. This would only help to encourage his distrust.

'I'm okay, Dad. I just needed to hear your voice. Is Mum there?'

'She's out walking the dog, but I can get her to call you as soon as she comes back. Why don't you come home for a bit? Just leave Cambridge a few days early.'

'I can't,' Tilly admitted, 'the police need me to stay around for some reason.'

Again, her father paused. 'Why? That's the daftest thing I've heard in a long time.' She imagined her father standing holding the phone with his chest puffed up. 'Why do you need to be stuck there without your family because he decided to kill himself? It's preposterous!'

For the first time since finding Dennis Wade's body it dawned on Tilly that perhaps it wasn't suicide. That would explain why the police needed her to hang around. The realisation did not sit well with her. 'I don't know, Dad, but I can't just run home every time something bad happens. I want to stand on my own two feet. I'll be okay, I promise.'

'Your mother and I can come to you. Just say the word.'

'Thanks, Dad. I'll be okay. Please get Mum to give me a call when she's back.'

'Of course I will.' She could hear the concern in his voice and began to regret making the call.

'I've got Yuki, remember. It's not so bad.' But in truth she wished she could jump in her small aging Ford hatchback and drive, without stopping, back to the comfort of home, her family and Ilfracombe.

'You call, if you need anything. Promise me you will. We love you.'

'I know. Thanks, Dad.'

'That's what dads are for.'

***

Back at Parkside Police Station, which overlooked the famous Parker's Piece where the first game of football with recognised rules was played, Elly Hale was busily tracking down the people who worked at the bookshop. The young sergeant, who was instantly recognisable because of the vampire red lipstick she wore, and her black-rimmed glasses, had been part of Barrett's team for a few years and was making a name for herself as someone who was hard working and diligent.

While she tapped away at her laptop, in between making calls, her brow was furrowed. This was the second largest murder case she had worked, and it concerned her that is was so soon after the Book Club Murders that the team had investigated only months earlier.

Thankfully that case had ended with an arrest, yet the trial had yet to begin.

Cambridge, from the outside, appeared to be a calm and tranquil place, but like any city it had its underbelly and Elly was gradually learning how grim it could be.

Although the Book Club Murders had involved violent crimes, this new case – and the missing finger of the shop manager – was not something any of them had come across before. As a result, despite the incident room being a flurry of activity, everyone was strangely quiet. It wasn't lost on Elly Hale that both cases were linked to the book world.

'Only in Cambridge,' she spoke to herself, under her breath, as she waited for the CCTV control room to answer the phone.

Eventually a gruff voice answered the call, 'Control room.'

'Hi, this is Sergeant Elly Hale from Parkside Police Station. We need you to send over footage from the camera on Trinity Street, near Ashton's Bookshop, from last night.' She checked her notes. 'From after 9pm up until 9am this morning as a matter of urgency please.'

'Will do. Might take a little while though.'

'I understand,' she said, although she didn't. 'If it would be quicker, I can send an officer over?'

'Nah, we'll get on it.'

Elly knew that the control room hated having CID peering over their shoulders and that as a result they would now spring into action.

'I appreciate it. Please send the file over to the major incident room. You have the email address?'

'Yeah, yeah, we've got it.' The man on the other end of the phone sounded bored.

'Great, thank you. We look forward to receiving it. Bye.'

Elly hung up and blew her dark brown fringe off her forehead. *Why were these things always like pulling teeth?*

After gathering some papers together, Elly straightened her pencil skirt and made her way towards Barrett's office, which was on the far side of the room overlooking the snow-covered green. From the window she could see families outside enjoying the snow and for a moment she felt a Christmas glow, but it was snuffed out as she opened the door to Barrett's office.

Her boss sat on his chair with his arms folded across his chest, glaring at the rest of the room.

'Sir, I thought you'd like to know we've managed to track down the address of Mr Wade's wife's sister.' Elly checked her notes, wanting to avoid eye contact. 'Mrs Francesca Woodcock lives in Yoxter, Somerset. I have a phone number; or will you be sending a car?'

'Call the Somerset local branch and tell them to send a squad car over to see Mrs Wade,' Barrett barked. 'We need her back in Cambridge as soon as possible. And we need the addresses of everyone who works at Ashton's.'

'Yes, sir, I'm working on it.' Elly excused herself and returned to her desk. She'd just about got used to Barrett's manner, but it didn't mean she appreciated it. Every single member of the team felt the pressure when a big case arose. She only wished he would be a little more polite.

On the other side of the room, Palmer and Sergeant Singh were trying to track down information about the main employee of Ashton's. What they had learnt was that Dennis Wade was not only the manager but also the owner of the shop. It had been in his family for nearly a century and he had taken over running it when his father had retired in the 1980s.

Palmer had given himself the task of contacting the company accountant, Marcus Goldman, so that they could check the financial situation the shop was in. Money was often a motive for murder.

DI Palmer sat back in his chair, clicking a biro as he searched the Internet for an address and number for the accounting firm, even though he knew he couldn't attempt to reach Marcus Goldman until the next of kin had been informed about the death. But Palmer wanted to have all his ducks in a row; so that once Mrs Wade had been told about her husband's murder, he would be free to crack on with talking to Mr Goldman. The same applied to everyone who worked at the bookshop. Being organised and ready was part of the job and half the battle. And although Palmer wasn't the most organised individual in the team, his desire to have the case wrapped up by Christmas meant that he was going to do his very best to be on top of such details.

After hanging up the phone to Broadbury Road Police Station police station in Somerset, Elly sauntered over to Palmer's desk. She'd always found him attractive and enjoyed his company. She knew only too well that he was a family man, but she figured a little bit of harmless flirting never killed anyone.

'Somerset Police have a local office to Yoxter, are they're going to talk to Mrs Wade,' Elly informed Palmer, while perching on the corner of his desk. He may have been ten years her senior, but she was not intimidated by him.

'Good. It will be a while before they can get her back to Cambridge, which is a pity.'

'Yes. Poor woman, having the news broken to her like that. Makes you feel grateful for what you've got,' Elly mused.

'It does indeed, sergeant.' Palmer scratched the light stubble on his chin while thinking about his eight-year-old son and wife, who were likely out in the fields by their house building a snowman.

'The finger is unusual,' Elly probed, wanting to hear if Palmer had any theories at this early stage.

'Very odd. The digit hasn't been found at the scene.'

'Do you think the killer took it with them?' Elly's eyes widened with horror.

'Too early to say, but…'

'You think it might be a trophy?' She realised where his train of thought was going.

'I didn't say that.' Palmer had a slight twinkle in his eye but kept a straight face.

'If it was a trophy then…' Elly let the statement hang in the air unfinished.

'Yes quite, sergeant. That is what I'm worried about.'

Chapter 4

By the time Mrs Veronica Wade had been delivered to the police station in Cambridge, darkness had fallen and the winter lights around the city shone a soft orange glow on the dense snow, making it sparkle like splinters of amber.

Mrs Wade, who had a round moonlike face, had small red eyes as a result of crying in the back of a police car for nearly four hours. By the time she arrived at the station she was exhausted. Her sister, Francesca, had accompanied her for emotional support. The similarity between the women was startling, and Barrett found himself wondering whether they were twins when he was first introduced to the ladies.

'Mrs Wade, I am terribly sorry for your loss.' Barrett, who had lost his own wife, had never been good at dealing with other people's emotions, but found his heart go out to the tearful woman in front of him.

She dabbed her eyes with a soggy handkerchief as she was led into a relatives' room to be interviewed.

'I just can't believe it.' Francesca had her arm around her sister. 'Dennis has gone. They were about to go on a cruise to celebrate their fortieth wedding anniversary. It's all so cruel.'

Barrett could see that Francesca was almost enjoying the drama.

'Take a seat.' He loosened his tie. It had been a long afternoon.

'You must tell me the details. The police in Somerset wouldn't tell me. What happened? Heart attack? I told him to watch his weight,' she sobbed.

Barrett and Palmer glanced and each other and Palmer readjusted his position in his seat, making the plastic beneath him creak.

'Mrs Wade, I am very sorry to tell you that your husband did not pass as the result of a heart attack. His body was found in Ashton's.' Palmer paused and cleared his throat. 'We believe that Mr Wade was murdered.'

The elderly women sitting opposite him both stopped, mouths open, and gasped.

'What do you mean, *you think*?' demanded the sister.

'We are almost certain,' Barrett said gravely, 'but we need to wait for the post-mortem to confirm.'

'Post-mortem?' Veronica's beady hazel eyes filled with tears. 'My Dennis on a slab?' Her hands began to quiver and she dropped her head to her chest.

'I understand this is an awful time for you, but I am afraid I have to ask some questions.' Barrett lent forward, resting his elbows on the desk between them.

'Can't you see she's in pieces?' Francesca pulled her sister into her bosom and glared fiercely at the inspectors.

'I understand this is a very difficult time, but a crime has been committed and it is our duty, and our job, to investigate.' Barrett had met women like Francesca Woodcock before. He knew that she was only trying to protect her sister, as well as exert her authority, but he had no time for her dramatic reactions.

'We won't keep you long, but we need some information to help us get a picture of what happened,' Palmer spoke softly. 'Mrs Wade, can you tell us when you last saw your husband?'

'She arrived to stay with me on Tuesday. She was meant to be coming back on Saturday evening.' Francesca spoke again for her sister.

'We need to hear it from Mrs Wade.' Barrett narrowed his eyes at the sister whose lips went into a thin line.

'Frankie couldn't be with us for Christmas. Her husband is sick, he has Parkinson's disease.' Veronica spoke with a croaky voice. 'I wanted to spend some time with them. I should have been coming back here on the fourteenth, not today. I wasn't supposed to come home today.' Her misery was tangible.

'So you left your house in Balsham on…' Barrett did some quick sums in his head. 'On the tenth?'

'Yes.'

'At what time?'

'Mid-morning. I said goodbye to Dennis as he left for work and then I packed and got ready to go.'

'What time did you arrive in Yoxter?' Barrett checked his notes.

'Probably around two.' Veronica dabbed her eyes again, her heavy mascara leaving trails across her cheeks.

'And you can verify this?' He turned to Francesca.

'I certainly can.' Her words were clipped. She had not liked it one little bit being silenced by him earlier.

'And on Thursday evening did you go out anywhere?'

Veronica looked over at her sister.

'No, we had dinner at home,' Francesca confirmed.

'And you were at your sister's house all night?'

'Why yes.' Veronica looked perplexed.

'You can confirm that?' Palmer asked looking over at Francesca.

'I most certainly can. We may live in the countryside, but I always lock the house up before going to bed. Only my husband and I have access to the key.'

'Right.' Palmer nodded at Barrett.

'Mrs Wade, can you tell me what sort of state of mind your husband was in on the Tuesday morning?' He closed his notes and cocked his head.

'Normal. He was just Dennis. He fed the cat…' She then paused. 'Oh, who is taking care of Cookie?' It dawned on Veronica that her beloved cat was all alone.

'We will take you home after the interview, Mrs Wade.' Barrett didn't like cats. 'You say your husband was normal, himself?'

'Yes. It was just a normal morning. Nothing unusual.'

'Did Mr Wade have anything he was worried about?'

'Well no. He always worried about the shop, he loved that place, but there was nothing out of the ordinary. He was fine.'

Barrett examined her response closely. 'Any financial worries?'

'No. None.' The woman was clearly offended by the question.

'Did he have any enemies? Anyone he had fallen out with?'

'No, for God's sake no. He was a good man. The best.' She buried her face in her hands.

'My sister has answered your questions. She needs to go home and contact her son.' Francesca rubbed her sister's back.

Palmer and Barrett gave each other a look and then both nodded, allowing Francesca to stand and help her sister out of her chair.

'We will arrange a car to take you where you want to go.'

'I'm afraid we will need to undertake a search of your home,' Palmer chipped in, knowing the distress that it would cause them. 'To help with our enquiries,' he added, hoping this would soften the blow but knowing it wouldn't.

As both women left the room, Palmer saw the look of distain plastered across Francesca Woodcock's face, but rather than acknowledge it, he turned his face to the ground knowing what an awful few months Mrs Wade had ahead of her. He found a small amount of relief when he heard the women muttering about checking into a hotel.

***

Back in the incident room, Barrett slammed his fists down onto his desk as Elly Hale delivered the news that the CCTV had given them no leads.

'We're going to find out if there is any CCTV on Sidney Street that covers the back entrance.' Elly spoke quietly, terrified of another outburst from her boss.

'This isn't the dark ages, Miss Hale. This is the middle of a busy city. Our killer must have been caught on camera. Find the image. I want it on my desk.'

In truth, Barrett liked Elly, but he was consumed with the job and often forgot to go easy on people, even those on his side.

'Yes, sir.' Elly jumped to attention and gladly made her way out of his office.

Palmer sat in a chair on the far side of the room strumming his fingers on his knee and looking out of the window as the city began to go to sleep.

'The wife didn't do it,' Palmer said.

'No,' growled Barrett, 'she didn't.'

'We will need to speak to the son. I ran a check on him…' Palmer closed his eyes, trying to remember the man's name. 'Andrew Wade.' He felt a pang of satisfaction. 'He lives in Peterborough. Born 1990. No spouse or dependents.' The rest he recounted from his notebook before checking his wristwatch and groaning. It was only nine o'clock and it looked like they had a long night ahead of them.

'The team are going to order some pizzas, sir. Do you want anything?'

'Get me some chips.' Barrett looked out over the city and wondered how the rest of the world could sleep so easy when there was so much darkness in the world. 'And ketchup. I need ketchup.'

'I'm on it.' Palmer stood and left the room, yawning as he closed the door behind him. That meant putting in a special order from elsewhere, as if he didn't have enough to do. As he picked up the phone and called the local kebab shop, he quietly cursed his boss under his breath.

Chapter 5

7.50am Saturday 14th December

Marcus Goldman was not in the slightest bit impressed when his home phone went and woke him up early.

'Yes,' he growled down the phone, unable to shake the sleep from his head.

'I would like to speak to Marcus Goldman,' an equally crotchety voice answered back.

'You are.' Marcus sat up in bed and cleared his throat, sensing the serious tone coming down the line.

'Mr Goldman, I'm DCI Barrett. I appreciate it is early, but I need to speak to you as a matter of urgency. I'm afraid that the body of Dennis Wade was discovered yesterday morning.'

Silence hung in the darkness of Marcus' bedroom. Suddenly the warmth from his duvet evaporated.

'Dennis? Dead?' Now that the accountant was fully awake, Barrett detected a slightly effeminate voice coming from the man.

'Yes. I understand that you were Mr Wade's accountant?'

Marcus rubbed his temples, trying to clear the whisky fog that had settled on his brain. 'I am, yes.' The information was not being processed as quickly as he liked. 'What happened to Dennis? Why are you calling me?'

'It would be better if we discussed this down at the station. Are you able to come in this morning, at say nine o'clock?'

'I'm not dressed,' Marcus said picking up his alarm clock and trying to make out the position of the hands in the darkness.

'You have time.'

Marcus didn't bother to argue, realising he had no say in the matter.

'Do I need a solicitor?' He suddenly felt under threat.

'Not unless you have done something illegal, Mr Goldman.' Barrett's words were spoken with a smile.

'Of course not,' the accountant protested.

'Very well. See you at nine.' And with that, Barrett hung up.

Marcus put the phone down gently, still trying to absorb the fact that his client and friend was dead. Whatever could have happened that meant the police were involved? He had a bad feeling in the pit of his stomach and he knew it was more than just a whisky hangover.

Slowly Marcus got out of his large double bed, which he slept in alone, and removed his burgundy satin dressing gown from the hook on the back of his bedroom door. Not yet ready to deal with artificial light, he made his way onto the landing and into the bathroom to shower.

He lived in Pinehurst, one of the finest residential apartment developments in the city. The 1930s building enjoyed communal grounds over which number 12 Grange Court, which belonged to Marcus, had lovely views. The second-floor apartment was light and airy and included an elegant sitting room with bay windows. It was decorated with antiques that he had collected over the years. The dining room had doors that led to the balcony, where he would often sit in the evening after work enjoying a measure of his favourite tipple, usually a single malt, while looking out over the sweeping lawns. In the winter months he took his evening drink sitting in front of the fireplace, while he read the paper and caught up with the news.

The previous night Marcus had entertained a young male guest, something he had done on numerous occasions. His sexuality, although obvious to most, was a secret he guarded. He had been brought up in an old-fashioned household.

While standing in the clean white bathroom, he observed his own reflection for a moment. There were bags under his eyes, set deep into his slender face. The whisky had taken control of him the previous night, as it so often did when he was entertaining. But most of the young, male companions who came to visit were people he'd met while walking along the river late at night. It was a good spot to pick up prostitutes looking for their next buck, in order to score their next fix. But Marcus was not an unkind man. He always treated his guests well and never expected them to do anything they weren't comfortable with. Still, having to live that part of his life in secret had taken its toll on him, and standing staring at himself he could see that as clear as day.

Wanting to bury the memory of the previous night's sordid encounter, Marcus ran a tepid shower and stood under the water, trying his best to wash away his sins. Had he known he was going to be spending his morning talking to the police about his dead friend, he would never have visited the river at eleven o'clock the night before.

The water could only wash away some of his guilt, and when he realised he was as clean as he would ever be, he admitted defeat and turned the water off.

Fifteen minutes later he was wearing one of his suits, complete with pocket-handkerchief and tie, and a single drop of coffee had yet to pass his lips.

Flicking on the kettle he checked his wristwatch. He had time to eat his usual breakfast, which consisted of half a grapefruit and a cup of black coffee. But on that morning, he didn't have much of an appetite, and even more unusual, he realised he wasn't looking forward to getting into his car. Marcus loved his MG but, on this occasion, he found himself wishing he could go back to bed. It was, after all, one of his days off. Or at least is should have been.

Discarding the grapefruit skin in the food bin, Marcus returned to his bedroom to check his appearance in the mirror one last time before leaving his apartment. It hadn't yet properly sunk in that his friend of fifteen years had died.

As he got into the driver's seat of his convertible, he checked his silver gelled hair in the mirror and made sure it was neat and smooth before he started the engine.

He drove through St John's College Playing Fields, past Magdalene College and across the river, making his way towards Jesus Lane, where his accounting firm was situated. Marcus had decided the detour was worth it. He wanted to gather the paperwork he had on Dennis Wade's business ready for his meeting with the police. Marcus was nothing if not organised.

As he removed the files from his cabinet and slipped them into his briefcase, a twinge of sadness hit him. Dennis may not have been the most exciting of characters, but he had been a good man – of whom Marcus was very fond of.

Frustrated by the one-way system, Marcus took eight minutes to get from his office to the police station. He arrived at three minutes past nine, much to his irritation.

When Palmer appeared to show Marcus to the interview room he was stuck by the man's smart attire. Apart from the solicitors who came and went from the station, Palmer was used to dealing with much scruffier people.

Barrett, who was holding a polystyrene cup of steaming hot coffee, joined them in the corridor.

Nerves getting the better of him, Marcus spoke before either of the detectives.

'Shocking news about Dennis. He was a fine man.' The accountant sat down and gripped his leather briefcase.

'Yes,' Barrett remarked coldly.

'What happened?'

'His body was discovered yesterday morning by a colleague in the bookshop. We are treating the death as suspicious.' Barrett slurped his drink.

'On my way here, I was listening to the radio. They said it was murder.' Marcus swallowed hard while Palmer and Barrett shared a glance.

'Yes. That's right,' Palmer admitted.

'Shocking,' Marcus repeated.

'How long have you known the deceased?' Barrett inquired.

'About fifteen years. I've been his accountant all that time, but I'd say he was more than just my client. I considered him a friend.' Marcus paused. 'I can't imagine anyone who would want to hurt Dennis. So, what was it? An unprovoked attack?'

'I can't go into any specific details about the crime,' Palmer told him, 'but we suspect the individual responsible knew the victim.'

Marcus felt cold and wished he, too, had a cup of coffee to wet his parched mouth.

'Can you tell us when you last saw the victim alive?' Barrett put his coffee down and slowly ran his finger around the rim of the cup.

'I couldn't tell you the exact date off the top of my head, but it must have been about two weeks ago. We had regular meetings regarding his accounts.'

'And did Mr Wade have any financial difficulties?'

'No, I wouldn't say so. He was hardly a millionaire,' Marcus confessed half whispering, 'but the shop made a reasonable profit and he was able to make a living. He owns the building, you know, so there was no rent on it. Only the usual business rates.'

'I see.' Barrett had found himself at another dead end and it had only just gone nine o'clock. 'Did he have any debts, any enemies, anyone who might want him dead?' The inspector knew he was clutching at straws, but he wanted to take something from the interview, no matter how small it may be.

Marcus sat back in his chair, looking slightly more comfortable and pondered the question. 'Not as far as I am aware.' He put his briefcase flat on the table. 'I brought his most recent accounts with me,' he added, gesturing to them, 'if you would like to see them.'

'That is very considerate of you, Mr Goldman,' Palmer said while contemplating whether the man opposite him might be gay.

'You say you were friends,' Barrett interrupted, 'so was there anything going on in his personal life that might have a bearing on the case?'

'We weren't that close.' Marcus looked down at his manicured fingernails. 'Occasionally we'd have a drink but most of our conversations centred round the bookshop.'

'What about his relationship with his wife? Were they having any problems?' Palmer could almost see smoke coming out of Barrett's ears as a result of his frustration.

'I only met her once or twice. She seemed like a decent woman. A homely sort.' Marcus almost sneered.

Women like that were clearly not his type, Palmer thought to himself, if women were his type at all.

'I didn't ask if you liked her, I asked you if they had any marital issues you were aware of.' Barrett was quickly losing control of his temper.

'No, Detective.' Marcus looked mildly offended at having been spoken to like that. 'I don't believe there were any problems there.'

Silence descended on the room like a fog for a moment while Barrett decided what to ask next.

Marcus spoke up, finding the silence too much to bear. 'He was a family man, a pillar of the community. People who went into the shop knew him and they liked him. He was respected. I can't imagine anyone who might have a grudge against him or would wish to do him harm. This whole situation is unfathomable.' He only stopped speaking when Barrett got up and left the room, disappointed not to have made any developments with the case.

'Thank you very much for taking the time to speak to us,' Palmer said, feeling embarrassed that Barrett had left without saying a single word.

'I am happy to help.' Marcus extended a languid hand and shook hands with the inspector.

'If we need anything else we will be in touch. In the meantime, might you leave the files you brought with you for us to look at? Some secrets are well hidden in plain sight.'

Chapter 6

Veronica and her sister had opted to stay at the Travelodge on Newmarket Road the previous night. Veronica, who now was more zombie than woman, couldn't stand the thought of getting into her marital bed alone, knowing her husband would never lie down beside her again. The women had called Veronica's neighbour, Peggy, who had a spare key to the house, and had asked her if she'd be kind enough to feed the cat, Cookie. Peggy, who was a lonely soul, had agreed but not without prying as to why the police had come knocking that morning. Thankfully Francesca, a woman who didn't pull her punches, had dealt with the nosy old woman effortlessly, much to Veronica's relief.

As they sat on their twin beds in the bland hotel room, Francesca brushed her fine dyed blonde hair thoughtfully. It had been less than twenty-four hours since she'd learnt of the murder of her brother-in-law, but she already felt more at peace with the situation. The same could not be said for her sister.

'V…' Francesca put her hairbrush back into her navy-blue handbag and turned to her sister. 'You really must speak to Andrew. He has a right to know.'

Veronica buried her face in her hands and let out a low moan. 'I can't. I just can't.'

'I know, dear, but you must.' She was quietly insistent.

'How can I tell my only son that his father is dead?' Veronica looked up, too exhausted to cry any more.

'You can't put it off. It's in the news already. If he hears it second-hand, he'll never forgive you. You'd never forgive yourself.'

The widow knew her sister was right, but she didn't know where to begin. Peterborough was only an hour away by train, but the distance had never felt so vast.

'V.' Francesca stood up, her broad figure doing a good job of blocking some of the cold light that was creeping through the curtains. 'The police want to talk to him. You have to be brave. Make the call.' She approached the phone that lay on the bedside table and handed the receiver to her sister.

With a shaking hand, Veronica dialled Andrew's number. After five rings it was answered.

'Hello.' The man on the end of the line sounded groggy.

'Andrew.' Veronica closed her eyes at the sound of her son's voice.

'Ma?'

'Yes, it's me.' She wanted to continue but the words escaped her.

'You sound odd.' Andrew coughed, feeling guilty that he still hadn't given up smoking, despite promising his mother that he would. 'Is everything okay?'

'I…' She could feel her throat tightening, and Francesca saw the terror freeze across her face.

'Ma, are you ok?' He wondered if she was calling for help. Maybe she needed an ambulance or something. But why would she call him?

When Francesca realised it was simply too much for her sister, she carefully took the phone out of her hand and put the heavy responsibility upon herself.

'Andrew, it's Francesca.'

'Aunt Frankie?' Andrew was now confused as well as nervous. 'What's going on?'

'I need you to sit down, Andrew.' Her words were calm but firm. 'I have to tell you something.'

'Sit down? Why?'

'Promise me you will sit down now, dear.'

'Fine, okay, I'm sitting down.'

Francesca wondered if this was true but had no option except to believe him. 'It's your father, Andrew. He… well, it's not going to be easy for you to hear this, but he's dead.'

The line fell totally silent and Francesca wondered if he'd fainted. 'Andrew, are you there?'

'What are you talking about?' The disbelief in his voice was tangible.

'I'm so sorry, young man. His body was discovered early Friday morning. He was found in the bookshop.'

'Of course he was.'

The flippant remark shocked Francesca. 'Do you understand what I'm telling you? Your father is dead.'

'Dead in the shop. Yes, I heard you.'

'This is no joke, Andrew, you understand that?' She couldn't fathom his reaction.

'No joke. Dad's dead. In the shop.'

It was Francesca's turn to fall silent.

'Well, I always said he'd rather die than leave work.'

'What did you say?' Francesca was horrified.

'You want me to pretend I'm upset? I won't. I won't do it. He was my dad only when it suited him. He loved that shop much more than he ever loved me. Everyone knew that.'

'This is no time for childish jealousy!'

'I'm over it, Aunt Frankie. Have been for a long time. I guess if he died in the shop then at least he died happy.'

Francesca was convinced Andrew hadn't absorbed the true reality of the situation. She paused for a moment and waited for him to speak.

But Andrew remained silent, still holding on to the phone. He looked around his small bedroom. The air was stale with a haze of cigarette smoke and on his bedside table sat an ashtray overflowing with cigarette butts. Beside that were some empty cans of larger. Andrew was pleased that the news had come via a phone call rather than as a result of his mother and aunt showing up. They would not have approved of his squalor and he did not have time for their disapproval.

'Is Ma alright?' Andrew finally broke the silence, while reaching for a half empty can to sip from.

'No, I wouldn't say she is.'

His aunt sounded clipped, but he didn't care. She'd made little effort with him when he was a child and the last time they'd seen one another was at the funeral of a distant relative. Andrew had never met the relative, but his mother had forced him to attend the funeral.

'Where are you both?' He drained the rest of the larger and scrunched the can up in his hand, hurling it across the room and aiming for an overflowing rubbish bin, which he missed.

'After speaking to the police your mother didn't want to go back to the house. She was staying with me when she received the news. We are staying in a hotel in Cambridge.'

'The police?' Andrew sat bolt upright, suddenly paying attention. 'Why the police?'

When she had first taken the phone, Francesca had been worried about breaking the news about the way in which Dennis had passed, but now, what with Andrew's total lack of distress, she said the words as if they were quite normal. 'Because he was murdered.'

***

In the incident room, Barrett paced backwards and forwards in his office waiting impatiently to hear news from the forensics team. Bob Roland, who had been at the scene, was the lead pathologist and had promised Barrett that he would be in touch.

By ten o'clock, when he still hadn't heard, he picked up the phone and dialled the number for the Addenbrooke's Hospital morgue department.

'Dr Roland.' The man who answered sounded out of breath as if he'd travelled some distance to reach the phone in time.

'Bob, it's Barrett.'

To Barrett's surprise, Bob Roland groaned.

'Ian, I was just about to call.' Bob was the only person who Barrett worked with who ever called him by his first name and Barrett didn't like it.

'Yes, yes, of course you were,' he said with a sarcastic grin. 'Any news?'

'Well, of sorts.'

Barrett didn't like the sound of that one little bit.

'You knew very well, it was going to be a nightmare. A public place, more DNA and fingerprints than you can shake a stick at.'

Barrett found himself chewing his lip in order to stop anything negative leaving his mouth.

'But.' Bob took a dramatic pause. 'There is some good news.'

Barrett let out a long slow breath.

'He was drugged. We've found Rohypnol in his system. The stomach contents confirm it was likely put into a drink. Probably tea.'

'Interesting.' Barrett had wondered how on earth the killer had managed to manoeuvre his victim into a position where hanging him would have been feasible.

'The other thing, which is not good news for our man, was that his finger was cut off when he was alive.' Bob wiped some sweat from his forehead; despite the fact it was minus one outside. 'Whoever is responsible doesn't have a brilliant knowledge of anatomy. The wound left behind was messy. I suggest some sort of saw was used. There are small abrasions around the skin that suggest it wasn't a clean cut.'

Although likely relevant, this wasn't the sort of information Barrett relished.

'Likely that the Rohypnol was in his system before the finger was removed,' Bob added, wanting to improve the situation. 'The removal of the finger likely took place when the man was suspended.'

Hanged, you mean, Barrett thought to himself.

'There was evidence that the killer cleaned the floor and the blood afterwards. Why? Well that's your department. The cause of death was asphyxiation, unsurprisingly.'

Barrett waited hoping there was more.

'That's it so far.' Bob wrapped up the conversation.

'Right.' The cogs of Barrett's brain were whirling. *Why remove the finger?* 'Well thanks, Bob. Keep in touch.' He hung up before the pathologist could respond.

'Hanging was cause of death. The finger was removed before he died. He had Rohypnol in his system.' Barrett reeled off the facts to Palmer as if he were reading a shopping list.

'Rohypnol?' Palmer's eyebrows rose. 'That, I was not expecting.'

'Unusual, I agree.'

'Flunitrazepam is usually proscribed for insomnia. It has ten times the strength of Valium, but it's easy and cheap to get hold of, so it's sometimes used as a parachute drug, to lessen the effects of coming down from other narcotics.'

'Presumably the drug was used so that the killer could get his victim into the noose.'

'That's what I'm thinking, Joe.'

'Hanging… it's pretty old fashioned.' Palmer picked at the skin around one of his fingernails. 'I mean, if you want to kill someone, there are easier ways.'

Barrett had turned his back to his colleague and watched as minute flakes began to float from the sky, promising to refresh the disturbed layer on the ground.

'What are you thinking?' Palmer asked the question before he had a chance to check himself. Barrett turned, a bemused expression on his face.

'This isn't couples counselling.' He smirked.

'Sir, we both know this isn't a crime of passion. It is premeditated. The killer thought about it. The body was left on display. It was almost theatrical. Our man…' He corrected himself. 'Our killer, is trying to tell us something.'

'This case has really got under your skin, hasn't it?' Barrett sat back in his chair and folded his hands behind his desk.

'No more than usual, sir.'

'Come on, Joe. What is it?'

Palmer considered this for a moment. 'I don't know. Something feels wrong. I don't like it. This crime feels like the start of something, not the conclusion.'

Chapter 7

Andrew drove, half-cut, along the A14 on his way from Peterborough to Cambridge in his ageing, dirty, white Citroen van, making sure he didn't once breach the speed limit. The last thing he needed was to be pulled over and breathalysed.

The traffic was slow, crawling at a snail's pace, as there was snow on the roads and a strong wintery wind battering the region.

He had the radio on for company but wasn't really listening. It was simply there to fill the silence and distract him so he didn't have to think about the situation he was heading towards.

By the time he arrived in Cambridge the snow was falling again, and the sky was a sheet of white.

He pulled his battered van into the car park and allowed himself a quick smoke before going in to the reception where, to his slight surprise, his aunt sat waiting for him.

'Andrew.' Her lips were pursed as she stood and approached him. There was no hug.

'Aunt Frankie.' He knew she hated being called that. 'Where's Ma?'

'Your mother.' Francesca corrected him. 'Is having a lie down. She's still in shock.'

'Right.' He scratched the back of his neck nervously and Francesca noticed how grubby his fingernails were.

'You could have showered,' she added with disdain. Andrew let out a sigh, already bored with her attitude. His tracksuit bottoms were also stained, and Francesca felt for her sister. What had she done to deserve such disrespect? 'Let's go and get a cup of tea, shall we.' She led the way to the restaurant, her navy-blue pleated skirt swishing around her broad hips as she walked.

The teenage waiter, who had some of the worst acne either of them had ever seen, took their order and skipped off, leaving the pair to talk.

'So…' Andrew scratched his neck again. 'Let me have what you know.'

Francesca recounted the events that had taken place over the last twenty-four hours with expert precision. She didn't miss out a thing.

'Someone strung him up?' Andrew had not been expecting that detail.

'It seems so.' She sipped her tea, uncomfortable with the truth. 'Your mother was too distressed to properly speak to the police yesterday. I'm not sure it is something she will ever want to talk about. It's cruel, just cruel.' Francesca shook her head.

'What have the police said?'

'Not much. They just wanted to know if he had any enemies, that sort of thing.' She fixed her nephew with beady eyes.

'What did you tell them?' Andrew felt a small sprinkling of sweat emerge on his brow.

'We told them he didn't have any,' she said steadily.

'Good.' Andrew leant back in his chair and picked at a bit of dirt on his well-worn trainers. 'That's good.'

'You should go to the station and speak to them. You might as well get it all out in the open. They will find out.'

Andrew folded his arms across his chest and cocked his head. 'What has my past got to do with this?'

'I just think the police will want to discuss it with you.'

'Why?'

'Because your father has been murdered and you have a criminal record.' There was no embarrassment in her statement.

'Oh, I see. Good old Andrew, black sheep of the family. He has a record so he must have done it. Do you know how fucking stupid you sound right now?' He spat the words across the table.

Francesca did not approve of bad language, and his vitriol left her feeling shocked and uncomfortable, so much so that she felt unable to speak for a few moments.

Andrew stood up. 'What's Ma's room number?'

'I told you, she's resting.' Francesca enjoyed exerting the small amount of power she had left.

'We may not have got on, but he was my dad. I have a right to see my ma. Which room?' He put his hands flat on the table and leant over his aunt.

'One hundred and five.' Francesca gave in, feeling intimidated by her nephew's tall frame. He was, if anything, rather skinny, but his height meant that he towered over her.

Andrew gave a sarcastic grin as a thank you and then left the restaurant and made his way towards the lifts.

***

At Parkside Police Station, Palmer came bursting in to Barrett's office like an over-excited puppy.

'Sir, I've just had a call from Mrs Wade's sister. She says we should speak with the son, Andrew. He's in the city now and he has a criminal record.'

'Send a car over to fetch him.' Barrett continued typing on his computer without looking up. 'And do it now.'

Andrew had only been with his mother for fifteen minutes before there was a knock on the hotel room door.

Veronica Wade, who was too distressed to get out of bed, remained lying there as Andrew opened the door.

Palmer stood holding his badge and introduced himself.

'We need you to come to the station and answer some questions.' Elly Hale stood side by side with her colleague.

'I just found out my dad's dead. How did you even know I was here?' He looked over Palmer's shoulder and saw Francesca standing there looking smug.

'Oh, I see, it's like that,' Andrew hissed at his aunt as he plunged his hands into his pockets, so that the officers wouldn't see he had balled his fists.

'I'm sure it won't take very long.' Palmer led the way along the corridor towards the lift. 'It's procedure to talk to the family. Nothing more.'

'Why do we need to do that at the station then?' Andrew was suspicious. He'd had dealings with the police enough times to know they couldn't be trusted.

Palmer pressed the button on the lift and chose to ignore the question. He had smelt alcohol on the man's breath and had taken an instant dislike to him. Andrew could suffer in silence.

***

Barrett ordered the printouts of Andrew Wade's criminal record and sat looking at the scruffy man opposite. He looked like he hadn't slept for several days, but Barrett knew it was the look of an alcoholic and drug user, rather than the appearance of someone suffering from insomnia. He'd had many dealings with petty criminals in his days before he was moved up to CID.

'Mr Wade, your history makes for some interesting reading.' Barrett's brown eyes fixed the interviewee.

'So I got a past, so what?' Andrew shrugged.

'Driving without a licence, possession of class A drugs, theft and assault.' Barrett read the list of convictions off with disapproval. 'A bit more than a past, I'd say.'

'You really are the lowest of the low, aren't you, Inspector? My dad is dead. Murdered. I'm grieving here, and there you are going on about my mistakes. It's a disgrace.'

'Pardon me, but you don't appear to be the grieving son you're claiming you are.' Barrett loosened his tie, letting Andrew know that he wouldn't be going anywhere any time soon.

'You don't know the first thing about me,' Andrew protested.

'I know rather a lot, actually.' Barrett tapped the file with his fingers.

'That doesn't mean anything.'

'The law would disagree,' Palmer interjected.

'The law is an ass!' Andrew said with a twinkle in his eye.

'If my father had been brutally murdered, I'm not sure I'd sit here making jokes,' Barrett growled.

'People deal with things in different ways. I'm not the crying type.'

'But you are the violent type, aren't you, Mr Wade?'

'That was then. I'm clean now.'

'Okay, but please explain why you were arrested in Peterborough on November sixth, carrying a baseball bat and herbal cannabis.'

'It wasn't mine.' Andrew folded his arms across his chest and shrugged.

'The magistrates believe otherwise. You were charged and released on conditional bail, were you not?'

'The case hasn't gone to court yet. My solicitor says the so-called evidence is weak.'

'I'm sure he did.' A small smile passed over Barrett's lips.

'Your bail was set at one thousand pounds. Where did you get the money from?' Palmer asked, looking at the suspect and concluding that the man didn't have a pot to piss in.

'I work. I've got a job.' Andrew wriggled slightly in his chair.

'What is it you do to make a living, Mr Wade?' Barrett couldn't wait to hear the answer.

'Odd jobs, here and there.'

Barrett suspected he knew exactly what that meant. 'So, you don't have full-time employment?'

'Like I said, I do a bit of everything.'

'And might that include selling drugs?' Barrett bit back.

'I'm clean. I told you,' Andrew sneered.

'Clean as of…' Barrett referred to his notes. 'November sixth?'

'It wasn't mine. Have you got cloth in your ears or something?'

Both officers knew that the interview was getting to Andrew. 'You still haven't explained where the money for your bail came from.' Palmer leant across the desk.

'A mate lent it to me,' Andrew eventually admitted.

'I can see from your record that, in the past, your father had posted bail. Why didn't you go to him this time?'

'None of your business,' Andrew hissed.

'This is a murder case. That makes it very much my business,' Barrett responded coldly.

'Well I didn't kill the old fool.'

'Can you tell us where you were in the early hours of Friday the thirteenth?'

Much to Barrett and Palmer's surprise, Andrew burst out laughing. 'Someone has a sense of humour.' Andrew shook his head still smiling.

'Why's that?' Palmer asked.

'Friday the thirteenth. It's funny.' He grinned and revealed crooked teeth.

'Does that date mean anything to you?'

'No more than it does to everyone else.' He shrugged. 'So…' Andrew unfolded his arms and leant in. 'Do you have any suspects?'

'We are exploring a number of avenues at this time.' Barrett cleared his throat.

'That means no.' Andrew smiled again.

'Tell me about your relationship with your father. When was the last time you saw or spoke to him?' Palmer changed the subject.

'Dunno. We didn't have regular cosy little chats on the phone if that's what you're asking.' Andrew looked down at his trainers and for a moment Palmer thought he saw a glimpse of sadness cross his face. 'He wasn't interested in me. We weren't close. I wasn't the son he hoped for. He only ever had time for that bookshop. I was an annoyance.'

'When did you last see him?' Palmer pressed.

'Maybe a couple of months ago.'

'Before or after your arrest on November sixth?'

'Before, I think. Mum insists on coming up to Peterborough and taking me out for lunch sometimes. We went to my local and had some food. They do good pies.'

The mention of food made Palmer feel peckish. He'd not yet had any lunch.

'What did you talk about?'

'Nothing much. This and that. I didn't do much talking and neither did Dad. Mum didn't have any problems filling the silence though. I ate my lunch and then got the hell out of there. Dad and I only agreed to do it for Mum's sake.'

'I see,' Barrett said as Palmer's stomach rumbled loudly around the interview room. 'You are free to leave now, Mr Wade, but I suggest you take a train home to Peterborough. I don't think drink driving when you are on bail is a wise move.' Barrett got up and headed for the door. 'I presume you had to hand your passport over as part of your bail conditions?'

'That's right.' Andrew suddenly looked fearful. He knew that if Barrett decided to give him a breath test he would fail and that would land him in prison.

'Good.' Barrett nodded with satisfaction as Andrew got out of his chair. He couldn't meet the inspector's eyes and that pleased Barrett no end.

'Don't go far, Mr Wade. We will be in touch.'

Chapter 8

Tilly had not slept well. The nightmares were almost alive, and she'd woken twice screaming. It was more than shock. She had absorbed the terrifying image of Dennis Wade hanging by his neck and it had seeded itself in her brain. And now that seed was growing, its roots taking hold of her consciousness and wrapping themselves around her skull.

She felt trapped in the flat, so she wrapped up warm, put her headphones in her ears and set off for a walk along the Backs. She needed to clear her head, and Tilly hoped that the cold wind would blow some of the cobwebs away.

Before she realised how far she had walked, Tilly found herself standing on the green looking at King's College Chapel, which stood proud with its two spires in the snow. *It's like a Christmas card image*, she thought, and for a moment, the horror trapped inside her head melted away.

Around her, tourists walked enjoying the architecture and the winter setting while the lyrics from a Nirvana song echoed in her ears. Between the buildings and the path lay the river, partially iced over, and above the powder blue sky framed the scene perfectly.

Tilly was enjoying the moment, up until the point where she spotted a man who looked like Dennis. He even walked the same way, with his head bent down as if he was inspecting the ground. The moment the stranger stepped into her line of vision the memory, of the rope cutting into the skin of his neck, returned.

She did everything in her power to push the image out of her mind but it didn't work. Instead she found herself thinking how odd it was that he didn't have his glasses on. He always wore glasses. Why were they missing? Where were they? Tilly realised that she needed to tell the police. She felt it was important, somehow.

Determined to turn her nightmares into something positive she set off towards Parkside Police Station, her large boots crunching through the snow.

***

Barrett and Palmer where just about to knock on the door of the house belonging to Jane Campbell, the other bookshop manager, when Barrett received a call from Elly Hale.

'What is it?' Barrett didn't like interruptions.

'News on the CCTV, sir.' She spoke quietly, trying to temper his mood. 'We can see that a hooded figure left the back entrance of the shop at nine minutes past four. We followed it as far as we could, but the person disappeared onto Jesus Green and we've not been able to locate where they exited after that. It appears that the figure is male but we can't be sure at this stage.'

'Did you say nine minutes past four?'

'Yes, sir.'

'Right.' Barrett's mind began to race. According to the pathologist, Dennis Wade had died sometime soon after midnight. What had the killer been doing in the shop all that time?

'We need more information on the figure spotted on CCTV. Get me height, approximate weight and anything else you can from the recording. I'm on Hobart Road. We are about to interview a Ms Campbell. I want that information on my desk when I return to the station.' Barrett hung up.

'Seems our killer spent a few hours in the company of the corpse, Joe.' He turned to face Palmer who had been listening to the one-sided conversation intently.

'Unusual,' said Palmer as Barrett knocked on Jane Campbell's green front door.

Jane lived in a small terraced house in the Romsey district of Cambridge, off Mill Road.

A skinny lady with frizzy brown hair opened the door cautiously.

'DCI Barrett. I'm looking for Jane Campbell.'

'I am she,' the woman said opening the door wider and letting the officers into her small living room. 'Excuse the mess.'

Palmer looked around, thinking it was an odd thing for Jane to have said. The place was immaculate. 'We are here because of the murder of Dennis Wade.'

'I realised that,' Jane said as she sat down on her petite navy sofa and folded her hands together in her lap. 'How may I assist you?' Despite the fact that Jane was unhealthily skinny, she was tall and carried herself well.

'We'd like you to tell us when you last saw Dennis Wade alive.' Palmer sat on an armchair opposite that matched the sofa.

'I was at work on Thursday. I did my normal shift and left at about half past seven, Dennis was in the building when I left. We said our goodbyes and that was that.'

'How long have you worked at Ashton's Book Shop?' Barrett asked. He had remained standing.

'Nearly ten years,' Jane said with surprisingly little emotion.

'Would you say that you and Dennis were friends?' Palmer inquired.

'We got on perfectly well. He was a nice man, with a good temperament. I wouldn't say we were friends. We were colleagues. Our relationship was strictly business.' Jane tucked a strand of her wild hair beneath her ear.

'Were you aware of any problems Dennis was having at work or in his private life?' Barrett was growing sick and tired of asking the question.

'None. Can I offer either of you gentlemen a cup of tea?' she asked checking her delicate gold wristwatch. Palmer guessed she was a creature of habit.

'Not for me.' Barrett wanted answers not tea. 'You do not seem particularly upset or surprised by the murder, if you don't mind me saying so, Ms Campbell.'

'I do not think it is appropriate to be emotional in front of strangers.' Jane played with a signet ring on her small finger. 'I was brought up better than that.'

'So there is nothing you can tell us that you think is of interest?' Palmer decided to try a softer approach.

'I don't want to get anyone into trouble,' she admitted biting her lip, 'but I did happen to overhear an argument.'

Barrett raised his eyebrows.

'It took place at some point in November. His son, Andrew, had called the bookshop wanting to speak to his father. When I handed Dennis the phone, he took it into his office and closed the door. I was rearranging one of the shelves nearby and heard his shouting a few minutes later. I wasn't eavesdropping, of course; it was hard not to hear what was being said. Dennis was clearly irate. I've never known him to lose his temper. It became apparent that Andrew was in trouble and asking for money. Dennis was refusing. Realising that this was a private matter I moved away from his office to the other side of the shop and got on with my business. I don't know how the call ended.'

'And this was in November, you say?' Palmer nodded, encouraging her.

'Yes, that's correct.'

'Thank you for sharing that information, Ms Campbell.' Barrett was now ready to leave. 'If you think of anything else that may be relevant to the investigation, do call.' He handed over a card with his number on it.

'As I said, I don't want to cause anyone any trouble. I'm just telling you what I know. It is my duty.'

'We appreciate your time.' Palmer got up from his chair and left the house with Barrett, leaving Jane sitting perfectly still on the sofa.

***

When the two men returned to the police station, Elly Hale was standing in the reception area greeting Matilda Edgely.

'Miss Edgely.' Palmer welcomed her with a smile and a nod of his head.

'Inspector.' She was slightly out of breath and her cheeks and nose were red. 'I realised something.' She stopped for a moment to catch her breath. 'His glasses, he wasn't wearing his glasses.'

'Who wasn't?' Barrett asked perplexed.

'Dennis. He always wore glasses, but I remember, when I found him, he wasn't wearing them. I only just realised. I knew something was wrong but I couldn't put my finger on it until now.'

Barrett and Palmer looked at each other. The young woman was right. Dennis had not been wearing glasses when they found his body.

'Thank you very much for letting us know.' Palmer shook her hand. 'You've done the right thing.'

'I want to help,' she said vulnerably. 'It's not right, what they did to him.'

Elly could see that Tilly was becoming emotional.

'You absolutely did the right thing.' Elly encouraged showing Tilly to the door and wanted to give the young woman a chance to get herself together before she left.

'We are getting somewhere,' Palmer said, following Barrett out of reception and up to the incident room.

'We are, Joe. Do you know if any glasses were found at the scene?'

'I don't believe so, but I'll call forensics and see what they bagged up.'

'Let me know when you've spoken to them. We also need to get Andrew Wade back again. He has some explaining to do.'

'Yes, sir,' Palmer said as he sat down at his desk and picked up the phone.

'I'll check with the wife. It's possible the glasses are at his home or something, but we need to find them.'

'Could our killer have taken them as a trophy?' Palmer asked holding the phone to his ear.

'Stop watching so much CSI on TV.' Barrett winked as he disappeared into his office to put in a call to Veronica Wade.

Chapter 9

'Right, here is where we are.' Barrett stood in front of his team, holding court. 'Dennis Wade seems to have had no enemies.

'We have CCTV footage of the perpetrator, who appears to be male, but this is yet to be confirmed. Dennis Wade died just after midnight, but the killer remained at the scene for four hours after committing the murder.

'Both the little finger, which was removed by our killer, and Mr Wade's glasses appear to be missing. His wife has confirmed that he would have had his glasses with him. They are not at his home and have not been recovered from the scene.

'His son, Andrew Wade, has a criminal record, with a history of assault. He is currently on bail. During his interview he told us he had not spoken to his father for some months – but a witness has confirmed that Andrew called his father wanting bail money, after his arrest on November sixth. We know that Dennis refused to help and this resulted in an argument.

'For now, Andrew Wade is our chief suspect. There is an arrest warrant being issued as I speak, and we will be bringing Andrew Wade into custody as soon as possible. Any questions?'

His team shook their heads and Barrett gave a nod to show his satisfaction before allowing them all to get back to work.

'Do we know where Andrew Wade is now?' Palmer looked tired. He rubbed his temples.

Barrett, for the first time in a long while, examined his colleague's face. Palmer was in his late thirties and had light brown hair, which he kept short. His blue eyes were framed with dark lashes and his chin was covered with well-kept stubble. Barrett noticed, for the first time, that Palmer's hair was thinning on the crown of his skull.

'Mrs Wade said he left Cambridge after the interview and likely returned to his flat in Peterborough. A squad car is waiting for the order to go and pick him up.'

'He's a nasty bastard.' Palmer was happy to admit. 'But do you really think he's our man?'

'In all honesty, Joe, I'm not sure. But he lied to us and he has no alibi. I think he knows more than he's letting on.'

'Sorry, sir, but I keep coming back to the finger.'

'What about the finger?' Barrett asked with a sigh.

'I can't see Andrew Wade sawing off his father's finger. He is violent but I don't think he's cruel. He has a temper and reacts. There is no evidence to back up the theory that he is the kind of man to plan such a dramatic murder.' Palmer almost instantly regretted saying this. He knew Barrett wouldn't like it.

'We'll know more when we interview him again. I wouldn't rule him out just yet.' Barrett's irritation hung on every word he said.

'Yes, sir.' It was Palmer's turn to sigh.

***

Back at her basement flat on Maids Causeway, Tilly was pacing up and down the small living area. Yuki, who sat on the sofa tucking into a steaming bowl of noodles, watched her flatmate with fascination. Tilly looked like a trapped tiger.

'What wrong?' Yuki asked with her mouth full; a dribble of broth ran down her chin.

'Why didn't he have his glasses? It doesn't make sense.' Tilly stopped pacing and turned to her friend.

'You must forget it. Police get killer. You no detective.' Yuki was already sick to death of listening to Tilly obsess over a pair of spectacles.

'But it's odd, don't you think? Why would someone kill a man and take his glasses? It's weird.'

'Yes weird. Killer weird.' Yuki sighed and balanced her empty bowl on the small cluttered coffee table. 'Let police do their job.'

Although Yuki was frustrated by Tilly's behaviour, she understood Tilly's need to focus on any detail other than the fact she had been the one to discovery the body of a murder victim. And that she knew the victim.

'You come sit. We watch X Factor final.' Yuki patted a spot on the sofa next to her.

Tilly, who was still thinking about the missing spectacles, agreed but knew she wouldn't be paying any attention to the reality TV show. She did it to please Yuki and because her body suddenly felt exhausted.

***

Palmer hated being the bearer of bad news, particularly when it came to his boss. He took his time to cross the floor of the incident room before entering into Barrett's office.

'Sir,' he said to the back of Barrett's head. His boss was sat in an office chair looking out of the window at the city lights. 'Andrew Wade was not at his address. His closet and wardrobe were practically empty. He's done a runner.'

Barrett didn't flinch. He sat totally still and didn't say a word.

'I am liaising with the Thorpe Wood police station and British Transport Police who are searching for his car.' Palmer sat down in the seat opposite Barrett's desk and put his head in his hands. He could feel a headache coming on.

'Is that all?' Barrett finally said, slowly spinning round in his chair to face Palmer who nodded silently, got up and left the room, closing the door behind him.

Chapter 10

T he courier removed the parcel from his van that was parked
on the icy pavement and approached the front door of
New Barn, Butcher's Hill, in the village of Ickleton.
It was cold and his breath puffed out of his mouth. He rang
the doorbell and waited. No answer. Keen to get back into his
van and out of the cold he knocked again, but still there was no
answer. Seeing that there was a light on upstairs, he walked around
the west wall of the converted barn and peered in through the
window.

The room was dark, but he could just make out the silhouette
of a body suspended in the air, lifeless. Dropping the package into
the snow, the Polish man ran back to his van, nearly skidding on
the ice, and put a call in to his boss to report what he had seen.
Half an hour later an ambulance and police officers were at the
scene.

Uniformed officers had been the first to arrive and break down
the door of the barn. Inside they had discovered the body of a
woman hanging from a beam. The rope was tied to the bathroom
door handle and, when the officer realised that the small right-
hand finger was missing, they put in a call to CID.

After racing to the scene Barrett and Palmer stood in the open-
plan living area of the barn looking at the corpse.

'Bugger,' Palmer said feeling sickened by the frozen expression
on the face of the victim.

'Our victim is Wendy Matlock.' Barrett turned to Palmer.
'The officers who had to break into the barn will have left their

bloody DNA everywhere. This is going to slow forensics down. Damn it.' He huffed. 'Where is Bob anyway?' He impatiently checked the time.

'I'm going to go back to the station,' Palmer told Barrett, who looked surprised that his colleague didn't ask permission. 'We need to get onto this right away.'

'Okay. I want the whole team looking into Wendy Matlock. This case has just taken a turn for the worse. See if you can find a link between the victims. Go back to square one and start from the beginning. Every piece of evidence, everything we know about Dennis Wade, needs to be looked at again with a fine-tooth comb.'

'On it,' Palmer said, grateful to be leaving the morbid scene behind.

'But, Joe,' Barrett called over his shoulder, 'I didn't say *serial*, you didn't say *serial*. Understood?'

'Yes, sir.' Palmer pulled his coat collar up around his chin and stepped out into the cold wind.

Barrett stayed in the barn examining the body. This victim was much younger than Dennis Wade. He knew that serial killers usually had a type and the two victims appeared to be almost opposite, but he suspected there would be something that linked them. His gut was telling him that this killer was sending a message rather than simply killing for twisted pleasure, and he believed the key to deciphering it lay in the method the murderer was using to kill. Why hang the victim? Why remove the little finger? Barrett knew that when he could answer those questions, he would be close to catching his killer.

Turning away from the body, Barrett walked around the open-plan living space the victim had once called home, inspecting the objects she once owned. On one of the walls hung pictures of Wendy, alive and well, enjoying various outdoor pursuits. There was a photo of her doing archery, another of her riding a horse and another of her hiking somewhere hilly. She looked happy and smiley in the pictures, nothing like how she appeared now. Her red hair was always tied up in the photos but had been worn down when she was killed. Strands of it hung over her face, obscuring one of her open eyes. Just like Dennis Wade, she had wet herself.

When Bob Roland appeared at the scene he did not look happy. He hated being called out on a Sunday, especially if it interrupted a premier league match he was watching on TV. Bob Roland was an avid Arsenal fan and as he took off his team scarf in order to get into his whites, Barrett smirked to himself.

'We've got another one, Bob. Same MO as Wade. Hanged and finger removed.' Barrett stood on the pavement below a large chestnut tree, its branches laden with snow. The sky was thick with snow clouds and the light was beginning to fade.

'Two one down when I left,' Bob muttered to Barrett, still stuck in football mode.

'Sorry to hear that.' Barrett knew very little about football and cared even less.

'So, you say it's the same as the bookshop victim?' Bob snapped into the job with effortless speed as he pulled on his overalls.

'Looks that way.' The inspector was rubbing his hands together trying to get warm.

'Let's take a look.' Bob led the way back into the barn. 'Have you identified the victim yet?'

'All the post out there is addressed to a Wendy Matlock. It would appear that she is our victim. If you can give me a time of death that would be great, Bob,' Barrett asked as Bob approached the body.

'I'd say she's been here for at least twelve hours,' Bob suggested. 'But I'll be able to confirm when we get her into the morgue. Who found her, Ian?'

'Some poor sod delivering a parcel. He called his supervisor in a panic and his boss called it in. Uniform have spoken to him and he's given a statement.'

Bob nodded and went back to working the scene in silence. The small serious look plastered on his face was one that Barrett had seen every time the pathologist had been called out to a crime. Barrett recognised the expression. It was one he often wore himself.

***

Francesca accompanied Veronica back to the house she had lived in with Dennis. The women got out of the taxi and both stood for a moment, looking at the exterior of 2 May's Avenue in Balsham. It was the first time Veronica had been home since learning of her husband's murder. Part of her longed for the comfort of home but part of her dreaded stepping indoors. That soon changed when the face of her cat, Cookie, appeared in the window meowing at them.

Veronica's eyes filled with tears as she turned the key in the lock on the front door. A pile of unread post lay on the doormat and the jiggling bell on the cat's collar sounded as the feline bounded towards her and greeted her in the hallway. She picked up her cat and snuggled her face in its fur, enjoying the familiar scent.

Meanwhile, Francesca bustled past making her way towards the kitchen carrying a bag of groceries they had picked up on the way from Cambridge. Francesca had always been the more practical of the two sisters and was determined to let Veronica grieve without having to worry about matters such as whether there was enough milk in the fridge. She felt powerless to do much else, but that was better than nothing.

Once both ladies had settled back into the house, the sisters sat at the kitchen table and had a well-needed cup of tea.

'It's good to be home,' Veronica said, wanting to assure herself as much as her sister. 'I feel closer to him here.'

'I can stay for as long as you need me. Doug can cope perfectly well on his own. The neighbours are keeping an eye on him.' Francesca referred to her husband who remained at their home in Somerset.

'Thank you, Fran.' Veronica rested her hand on top of her older sister's.

'That is what families are for.' Francesca removed her hand and put it in her lap. She had never been very comfortable with public displays of affection. 'So...' She glared at her sister. 'What are we going to do about Andrew?'

'Honestly, I don't know what to think.' Veronica's face fell at the mention of her son's name.

'It doesn't look good, him going missing like that. Did you know he had been in trouble with the police again?'

'No. I had no idea. Dennis didn't tell me.' Veronica said a silent thank you to her husband for keeping the secret from her. She had grown tired of hearing about Andrew's clashes with the law and had come to the conclusion that what she didn't know couldn't hurt her. But her blissful ignorance had been sadly short lived. 'It doesn't look good,' Veronica had to agree.

'Why run? Unless he's guilty of something.' Francesca let the statement hang in the air.

'They didn't get on, but Andrew would never hurt his father.'

'He's hurt others though, hasn't he?' Francesca had given up on Andrew a long time ago.

Unsurprisingly, his mother was determined to defend him most of the time. But since his disappearance a doubt had seeded itself in her mind. What was Andrew capable of? She wasn't sure she knew him at all.

'The police won't give up until they've found him. Stupid boy, running away like that. He can't hide forever.' Francesca's statement shocked her sister.

'You think Andrew is responsible?'

'I think the police think he is,' said Francesca reining in her opinion.

'Well, I think they are clutching at straws. My Andrew has made mistakes but he's a good boy underneath it all.'

Francesca sipped her tea and kept her lips buttoned. It wasn't her place to burst her sister's bubble, especially given that she had just lost her husband too.

***

Palmer hung up the phone at Parkside Police Station, having just spoken to the British Transport Police about the whereabouts of Andrew Wade. It seemed his car had been spotted on CCTV heading south on the A1 towards London. Later the car was seen turning off towards Luton and a few hours later they had tracked it, using camera footage from Saturday afternoon, all the way down to a spot near Basingstoke in Hampshire.

'Shit,' Palmer said to himself as he approached Elly Hale's desk.

'Everything alright?' She looked up at him over her glasses.

'Andrew Wade. Seems he was headed to Portsmouth, most likely so the little runt could get a ferry, I suspect. I need you to get onto border control and see if they have any record of him leaving the country in the last twenty-four hours.'

'Yes, sir.' Elly Hale sprang into action. She loved the chase, which the job provided.

'Singh!' Palmer beckoned the sergeant over. 'I need you to get me as much background information as you can on a Mrs Wendy Matlock. Here's the address,' he said handing over a scrap of paper. 'I want details from you as and when they come in.'

Singh nodded and shuffled back to his desk on the far side of the incident room to get on with his work. Looking up at the clock on the wall Singh knew he'd be lucky if he made it home before ten o'clock that night. The team had a long afternoon ahead of them, which was never good news, especially on a Sunday.

Chapter 11

Tilly woke drenched in sweat. It was as a result of the same reoccurring nightmare she'd been having since discovering the dead body of Dennis Wade. Her hair stuck to her forehead and the fabric of the T-shirt she wore in bed was plastered to her back.

Once her heartbeat had settled, she lay back down feeling exhausted and buried her face into her damp pillow, instantly regretting the decision.

Meanwhile, across the city, Palmer was waiting to interview another Ashton's Bookshop employee, while Barrett worked upstairs in the incident room trying to build a better picture of Wendy Matlock's life.

Palmer and Singh greeted Steven Fisher in reception and led the man to the interview room. He was slightly surprised by Steven: he had been expecting someone a bit younger. The men sat down opposite each other at a table and Palmer ran his eyes quickly over his notes.

'Thanks for coming in to talk to us, Mr Fisher. Let me assure you this is all just procedure.'

'No problem, happy to help,' Steven said knitting his fingers together. 'I still can't quite believe it. You don't expect that sort of thing in a place like Cambridge. Folks round here believe it's a safe place. Well, they did until Mr Wade, of course.'

'Yes, we are dealing with a particularly violent crime,' Singh agreed.

'So, what do you need to know?'

Palmer found it refreshing having someone cooperate in an interview. Most people were less forthcoming. 'I have here a table of the hours everyone employed by the shop worked last week. Can you confirm this is correct?' He slid the piece of paper across the desk.

Steven's large smooth hand reached out and examined the timetable. 'Yes, that's all right. I worked those days.'

'So, was your Wednesday afternoon shift the last time you saw Dennis Wade alive?' Singh inquired.

'Yes.' Steven looked ashen. He had a skinny face that was semi-covered by a dark beard, which made his bright green eyes stand out.

'How long have you been working at the bookshop?'

'A few months. Since September time. I've been travelling for the last few years. I didn't want to go straight back into full-time work, so the hours suited me.'

Palmer could see that Steven looked like he'd been backpacking. The worn leather band he wore on his wrist and the slightly dishevelled hair now made sense.

'Where are you living?' asked Singh.

'My mother, Georgia, died unexpectedly while I was travelling. I came back to arrange the funeral. I was her only child. I never knew my dad. Mum said he wanted nothing to do with us. She never even told me his name.' Steven paused, looking lost for a moment, before regaining his composure. 'Mum left me her house off Chesterton Road, near the river. It's fine for now but I think I'll sell up and use the money to travel again. I've got the bug a bit.'

'Sounds nice.' Palmer imagined himself living such a carefree life and realised it would never have suited him. He loved the job and wouldn't swap his family life for the world.

'After Christmas has been and gone I won't have anything to keep me here,' Steven continued. 'Without Mum, and what with the shop being closed for now, I think I'll put the house on the market in January and get the hell out of this ice bucket.' He winked and Palmer found himself warming to the man. 'Give me the sunshine any day. Bondi Beach is my idea of heaven. Spent a good few weeks there back in 2017. I might open up my own bar. Always thought that would be a nice life.'

As Palmer listened to Steven, he came to the conclusion that the man was a daydreamer.

'Right, well, thanks for coming in and speaking to me.' Palmer cut in wanting to get back to doing something that might help with the case. 'Just one final question. Do you know a Mrs Wendy Matlock?'

Steven wrinkled his brow searching his memory. 'Nope. Doesn't mean a thing to me. Why?' he asked looking suspicious.

'Just another line of enquiry we are pursuing.' The lie rolled off Palmer's tongue with ease.

'Is she a suspect?' Steven half whispered leaning across the table, encouraging Palmer to share information with him.

'I'm afraid I can't comment on that at this time.' After saying it he wondered how many times in his career he had used that exact phrase.

'Fair enough. Got to play your cards close to your chest, Detective. My mum taught me that.' Again, he winked.

'If anything occurs to you that you think might be relevant to the case, do call,' Palmer said handing over his card and shaking hands with Steven. 'Sergeant Singh will show you the way out. Thanks again.'

Returning to the incident room, Palmer was about to go and file some paperwork regarding a crash that had taken place the previous week on the M11 when he was waved over by Barrett. He was leaning over Elly Hale's desk looking at something she wanted her boss to see.

'We have footage of Andrew Wade getting onto a ferry at Portsmouth harbour. The video recorded the time as 9.33 on Sunday morning. The ferry left the dock at ten o'clock and landed in Cherbourg at one in the afternoon. I have been in touch with Interpol and they are on the look-out for his vehicle, but he has a head start on them, sir. They are checking AutoRoute CCTV as we speak.'

'Slippery little bastard,' Barrett said, referring to Andrew Wade, as he turned to face Palmer. 'I want to see you in my office.'

Following his boss, Palmer worried that he'd done something wrong. He wracked his brain to try and work out what that might be.

'Close the door,' the DCI barked as he took a seat in his chair.

'I've had the Chief Constable on the phone to me this morning. He's had the press on his case. Seems someone has let slip about our second victim.'

'Well it wasn't me, sir!' Palmer held his hand against his chest in horror.

'I know that, Joe.' Barrett softened, and Palmer breathed a sigh of relief. 'Could have been the courier. Anyway, point is, it doesn't matter who it was. What matters now is that we have a media storm brewing and the Chief Constable isn't too happy about it.'

'It won't help the investigation,' Palmer agreed, sitting down and allowing himself to relax a little.

'No, normally I would agree with you but in this instance, I think we have an opportunity.' There was a twinkle in Barrett's eye that Palmer hadn't seen for a long time. 'The truth is, Joe; this murderer has killed two people in as many days. It is too early for us to have uncovered the pattern and we are at the mercy of this criminal. Rather than try and bury the story, why not use it to our advantage. We could do a reconstruction, for example. It's worked in the past.'

Palmer thought about this for a moment. 'The Chief Constable will never allow it.'

'I suspect that the Chief Constable doesn't want any more people found hanging with their fingers removed, either!' Barrett spat. 'If our killer is prepared to strike twice in such close succession, who knows how long it will be before another victim shows up...'

Palmer spent the rest of the morning filing his report on the crash that had taken place the previous Monday. The hazardous weather had instigated the problem and a lorry had lost control on the ice, careering into a number of cars before ending up tipped over on the side of the road. There had been no fatalities but three people had been seriously injured. It was an open and shut case but that didn't mean there was any less paperwork, and cuts to the budget meant that every single officer was spread very thinly across a number of on-going investigations. It was a part of the job they all resented but something they couldn't control.

By lunchtime the DI was feeling bad tempered and took himself outside for some fresh air. The incident room could get very stuffy, even if the temperature outside was only three degrees.

As Palmer stood on the pavement overlooking Parker's Piece, he watched a young family trying to make the best of the now grey-brown slushy snow. Their attempts to build a snowman were hopeless.

The large square green had looked so pretty when the snow had first landed. Now it was turning into a dirty bog. Palmer sank his hands into his coat pockets and turned his back on the view. The sight of the filthy snow had done nothing to lighten his mood at all. As he made his way up the stairs to the incident room, which was at the top of the building on the fourth floor, he hoped that the team had found some useful information that would shed light on the case.

Much to his pleasure, when he opened the door to the large open-plan incident room, he discovered a flurry of activity. Had he missed something in those few moments he'd spent out on the street? Wanting an answer to his question he went over to Elly's desk and asked her what all the excitement was about.

'Interpol have been in touch. They think they have a lead on Andrew Wade. It seems he crashed his car into a tree somewhere along the AutoRoute heading in the direction of Tours. Local police found the car abandoned. There's been heavy snow in France, too, apparently. It appears there is some blood on the steering wheel and some on the driver's side of the windscreen. French police are mounting a search of the area as we speak.'

Her dark eyes smiled with excitement and Palmer's bad mood quickly melted away. Finally, it looked like luck might be on their side.

'Good news.' A satisfied smile lit up Palmer's face. 'I'm still not convinced he's our man, but he ran and he lied, so we will need to talk to him again. Let me know the minute you hear anything else from Interpol.' Palmer patted Elly's shoulder and went to deliver news of the development to his boss.

'Okay.' Barrett listened to the information with a frown on his face.

'What is it, sir?' Palmer asked.

'He could not have been responsible for victim number two. Either we have a copycat, which seems extremely unlikely given that the information regarding the removal of Dennis Wade's finger has been kept out of the press; or Andrew Wade isn't our man.'

'Agreed. But he is hiding something, and it might be significant to the investigation.'

'Quite,' Barrett said sharply.

'There are two things I want to mention. We now know that our killer strikes at night. The lights have been off in both instances so the killer left the bodies hanging in the dark. Secondly, it's quite clear that the victims have been studied by the murderer. The killings took place when the killer was sure they wouldn't be interrupted. This takes time and patience. He or she must have stalked Wendy and Dennis.'

'Or worked his way into their lives,' Barrett added thoughtfully.

'Exactly.'

'How did the interview go this morning?' Barrett changed the subject wanting to give it more thought before discussing it further.

'He wasn't any help. Nice bloke, though.'

'Right. I want you to gather together all the information we have on Wendy Matlock. Perhaps the key to understanding our killer's motive lies somewhere there.'

'I've been giving some thought to your idea about involving the press. I think at the very least we should make a statement warning the public to be vigilant. The Chief Constable will approve of that much, I'm sure. And we could slip a few select bits of information into the statement that could help with the search for the killer, and perhaps throw up material that might aid the investigation.'

'I'd been thinking something similar myself, Joe.'

'I'll contact the press and arrange a conference.'

Chapter 12

Veronica hung up the phone and went and sat quietly in a chair. Her face was ashen, and her sister could instantly tell something was wrong.

Francesca crossed the room and went and stood next to her sister, bending over to take hold of her hand. 'Whatever is wrong?' She could tell this was something else, something other than grief.

'That was the police.' Veronica stayed seated, looking past her sister staring into the distance and not blinking.

'What did they say?' Francesca did not like the expression on her sister's face. It made her feel uneasy.

'They found another.'

'Another what?'

'Another body.'

Those two words had the magical ability to silence Francesca.

'A woman.' Veronica's voice was hoarse.

'A woman?' Francesca finally spoke, her words filled with horror

'A woman,' Veronica repeated.

'When? Where?'

'This morning in a village outside the city.' Still Veronica remained unblinking.

'A woman.' Francesca was rehashing the details of Dennis's murder through her mind. How he had been hanged, the fact his finger had been cut off. It was horrific but the thought that the same thing had happened to a woman, even if she was a stranger, made her stomach turn. 'Was she killed in the same way?' Francesca had to know.

Veronica simply nodded while her sister shut her eyes trying to block the awful thoughts and images from entering her head.

'Andrew,' Francesca said all of a sudden.

Veronica turned to face her sister with a perplexed look on her face. 'He wouldn't.' But all of a sudden, she didn't feel so sure.

'He's in big trouble this time. This isn't smoking marijuana or beating up some man in a pub. This is serious.'

'It was serious when Dennis died.' Veronica reminded Francesca, and picked at some fluff on the side on the armchair she was sat in.

'But that was a crime of passion,' Francesca suggested. 'This is something else.'

'He didn't do this.' Veronica shook her head and got up, putting distance between herself and her sister. 'You may not believe him, but I expect you to believe me. Andrew had nothing to do with this. You'll see.'

'The only way that can ever be proved is if he hands himself in or the police catch him. As long as he is on the run it doesn't look good. You must see that?'

'I am going to respectfully ask you to drop it.' Veronica glared at her sister. 'He is my son. Remember that.'

Francesca, who was not used to having Veronica stand up for herself, pursed her lips and nodded. Veronica could request that she remained silent, but she did not – and would not – control what Francesca thought; and Francesca was still convinced that Andrew had something to do with the murders. Veronica had always been naïve and this, in Francesca's mind, only went further to prove it.

'I fancy some fresh air,' Francesca called out to her sister as she slipped on her coat and slammed the front door shut. She was angry that after everything she'd done for Veronica, she was being treated so badly and opted to spend time wandering around the cold empty village rather than be inside with her sister in the warm.

As she made her way, slowly and carefully, along the slushy streets of the village, Francesca found herself thinking about Andrew. She couldn't understand where his life had gone so wrong. He had been a happy boy, loved by his parents. It was true that Dennis had never been especially good with his son but equally he'd never done anything to hurt him. It simply didn't make any sense.

All she did know was that Andrew started on this dark path when he was about eleven years old. The boy changed from being a happy-go-lucky lad to a withdrawn, sulky little brat. Francesca had always put it down to hormones, but given recent events began to wonder if there had been more to it than that.

She searched her memory to see if she could pinpoint an event that might have caused the change in Andrew, but nothing stood out and she found herself feeling even more frustrated and helpless. Neither were emotions she relished, or dealt with well, and as she turned the corner and saw the church, she decided the only thing left to do was to pray.

***

DI Palmer was not a man known for losing his temper but, after the team had trawled through Wendy Matlock's past without finding any link between her and Dennis Wade, he had shouted, sworn and walked out of the incident room. He had left some shell-shocked colleagues in his wake.

What they had discovered was that Wendy was married but separated from her husband. Wendy had married Shane Matlock in 2010 and the couple had parted ways in mid-2017. Shane Matlock had moved out of the marital home, in which Wendy had remained living in, up until her murder. After looking into her finances, the team had also discovered that Shane still contributed to the mortgage payments, despite the fact the couple had no children and had never legally divorced.

Once they knew Wendy had been married, Singh had been tasked with tracking down the victim's husband. The man was now living in Royston, a town in north Hertfordshire, about fifteen kilometres south west from Cambridge. It seemed Shane ran a construction company and was now living with a woman called Gemma Nash in a rented house on the Gower Road, a quiet street on the north side of the town.

When Barrett heard about this, he had called Palmer and ordered him to take Singh and go to Royston to break the news to Shane. Frustrated by the lack of progress at the station, Palmer was pleased to be given an opportunity to get out.

The DI and the sergeant drove in silence to Royston. Palmer was still in a foul mood and Singh decided that remaining tight lipped was his best bet.

As the distance between the car and Cambridge grew the snow on the fields appeared cleaner again. The slush, like Palmer's irritation, was gradually disappearing.

Pulling onto Gower Road, Singh kept his eye out for Hawthorne cottage and soon saw it on the left and pointed it out to Palmer, who pulled the car up onto the pavement.

Getting out of the driver's seat, Palmer proceeded to put his foot into a deep cold puddle of slush. As quickly as his mood had lifted the cloud returned. No officer ever liked having to break the news of someone's death to their next of kin, and this was no exception.

After knocking on the brown front door of the small brick semi, Singh heard the sound of footsteps approaching from inside.

To their surprise a woman in her twenties opened the door. She had perfectly applied make-up but too much of it, as far as both men were concerned.

'Can I help you?' She spoke with an Essex accent.

'We need to speak to Mr Shane Matlock. Is he here?' Palmer flashed his badge and noticed the look of surprise on her face.

'I'm his girlfriend Gemma.' She rested her hand on her small pregnancy bump to emphasise the point. 'Is he in trouble?'

'Is he here?' Palmer ignored her question looking over her shoulder into the small house.

'He's having a nap. He had a late night with the lads.'

Stepping past her into the poky living room, Palmer told the woman she needed to go and wake her boyfriend up.

Reluctantly agreeing, Gemma climbed the stairs leaving the officers alone downstairs.

'It's small isn't it,' Palmer commented, thinking about the difference between the house they were in and the spacious barn Wendy Matlock had lived in.

Singh nodded, thinking it wasn't that different in size from the place he rented in Cambridge.

When Shane finally appeared he looked worse for wear. He had dark bags underneath his eyes, unkempt stubble and messy hair. He wore a checked shirt and jeans.

Extending a hand to introduce himself to the officers he looked rather embarrassed.

'Mr Matlock, sorry we woke you,' Singh apologised, 'but I'm afraid we have some bad news.'

At hearing those words, Shane looked even paler than he had done when he first joined them in the living room.

'I am sorry to tell you that we were called out to New Barn on Sunday afternoon after a body was discovered by someone delivering a package.'

Shane sat on the sofa, dreading what was coming, but waiting for his fears to be confirmed.

'We have confirmed that the deceased was Wendy Matlock. I am very sorry.'

Gemma went to her boyfriend, put her arms around him and held him tight.

'How do you know it's Wendy?' Shane croaked.

'Dental records confirmed the identity,' Singh volunteered.

'How did she die?' Gemma was clearly dismayed. The officers looked at each other.

'It is being treated as murder,' Palmer said gravely.

'Murder?' Shane looked horrified. 'How? When?' The man was obviously distressed but was somehow managing to control his emotions.

'Can you tell us where you were on Saturday evening?'

'He was here with me,' Gemma cut in quickly.

'Did you go out at all?' Palmer continued to direct his questions at Shane.

'Only to pick up something for Gem.'

'How long were you gone for?'

'Maybe fifteen minutes. No more. I just went to the shops. Gem keeps getting cravings for baked beans and we'd run out.' The man buried his face in his hands.

'I know this is a difficult time for you, but I do have some more questions.' Palmer spoke more gently. 'Can you tell me when you and Wendy separated?'

'About eighteen months ago.' Shane's face stayed in his hands. Gemma stroked his back in a soothing motion.

'Can you tell me why the relationship ended?'

'Why do you need to know this? I've told you I was here. Gemma was with me. What's my failed marriage got to do with anything?'

'We need to build a clear picture of the victim.'

'They couldn't have kids.' Gemma spoke, wanting to save her boyfriend the heartache of having to rehash his painful past. 'They tried for years but it just never happened. It was difficult for both of them.'

'Who initiated the split?' Palmer made notes on a small pad, which he'd removed from his coat pocket.

'It was a mutual decision.' Shane looked up. 'We loved each other, but when we gave up on trying to get pregnant… we grew distant. We'd been trying for nearly seven years and when Wendy decided she couldn't face any more disappointment she just shut down. I tried for a while, but I've always wanted to be a dad. She knew that, but she gave up on the idea. She spent more and more time at work and threw herself into her hobbies. I just couldn't cope with the idea of a future without children. So we broke up and I moved out.'

Palmer watched as the new couple held hands. 'Can I ask how long the two of you have been together?'

'We met about six months after I moved to Royston.'

'I'm five months gone,' Gemma told Palmer while rubbing her belly and pre-empting his next question.

'I see.' Palmer shut his notebook and slipped it back into his pocket.

'I'm sorry.' Shane shook his head. 'But I need to digest this. Can't we do this later?'

'We will have more questions for you,' Palmer admitted, 'but I have only a few more for now then we'll leave you in peace. Mr Matlock, can you tell me if Wendy had any enemies? Anyone who you can think of who might wish her harm?'

'Wendy?' Shane half laughed. 'She wasn't that type. She was a gentle woman. She wouldn't hurt a fly.'

'So you were in regular contact with her?' Palmer's eyes narrowed, and he watched as Gemma tensed.

'I wouldn't say that.' Shane shifted on the sofa. 'We remained on friendly terms.'

'When did you last see her?'

'Maybe a few weeks ago. Some post for me had been delivered to the barn. I went to collect it.' From her reaction, clearly this was news to Gemma.

'And when you visited Mrs Matlock, she didn't mention anything that might be significant?'

'She gave me the post, then I left.' Shane could feel his girlfriend's anger bubbling.

'Okay. That will do for now.' Palmer indicated to Singh that it was time to leave. 'We may need you to come down to the station and answer more questions.' Shane nodded meekly. 'Thank you for your time.'

***

Back at Parkside Police Station the press were gathering and waiting for Barrett to appear to make a statement. The room was buzzing with conversation and Barrett watched all the reporters through a crack in the door. He was comfortable standing up in front of his team but talking on cameras was well out of his comfort zone.

Elly Hale sat nervously at a desk laid out in front of the cameras and microphones. Much to her horror she had been asked to introduce her boss to the press. When she spotted Barrett peering through the door, she knew it was her signal.

'Good afternoon.' Elly's voice was shaky. She cleared her throat. 'Thank you for joining us. DCI Barrett will be speaking in a minute. We request that you don't ask any questions until he has finished his statement.'

The room fell silent and all eyes turned to look at Elly. Below the desk she clenched her hands together wanting to sink down into her seat and for the ground to swallow her up. Seconds later, much to her relief, Barrett walked into the room and took his seat next to her.

'I'd like to thank you all for coming at such short notice.' He pulled at the lapels on his navy-blue suit jacket, as a physical signal to exert his authority.

'At approximately three fifteen on the afternoon of Sunday the fifteenth of December, officers attended an address in Ickleton and discovered the body of a woman at the address. The deceased, a Mrs Wendy Matlock, age thirty-nine, was pronounced dead at the scene. This case is being treated as murder. We would request that anyone in the area of Butcher's Hill, in Ickleton, on Saturday night please come forward.' Barrett looked at the faces of the people watching and recording him.

'We believe that the murder of Wendy Matlock and that of Dennis Wade, who was discovered in Ashton's Bookshop on Friday morning, are linked. On behalf of the officers, I wish to pass on our sincere condolences to the friends and family of both victims at this terrible time. I urge anyone who has any information about either of these vicious crimes to contact detectives or call Crimestoppers.

'We ask that the general public remain calm but vigilant at this time. Thank you.'

Barrett sat back and watched as a vast number of hands sprung up into the air. 'Yes.' He pointed to a man who sat in the front row.

'Is it true that both victims were discovered hanging?'

Whispers travelled around the room.

'I am not prepared to comment on that at this time.' Barrett turned his body slightly and pointed to a woman standing at the back of the room.

'Is there a link between the victims?'

'At this stage we are exploring all possible avenues.'

'Do you have any suspects?' another reporter called out from somewhere in the audience.

'Currently, we do have someone of interest who we believe will be able to assist in our enquiries.'

'Who?' shouted someone else.

'I am not prepared to comment at this time.'

'Are the police considering the idea that a serial killer may be responsible?'

'There are similarities in the method in which both victims were killed.' Barrett had to be very careful how he worded himself. 'We are keen to trace a man recorded on CCTV who was in the area near the bookshop in the early hours of Friday the thirteenth. The man was spotted walking towards Midsummer Common wearing a dark hooded jacket. If anyone has information about this person, we request you come forward so that we can eliminate this male from our enquiries.'

Another question. 'I understand that a warrant has been issued for the arrest of Andrew Wade, the first victim's son. Can you tell us if he's a suspect in the case?'

'I can confirm that Andrew Wade is a person of interest at this time and we are keen to talk to him further.'

Mutters travelled around the room in ripples as Barrett got up and excused himself, letting out a deep sigh of relief once he'd shut the door behind him, leaving Elly Hale in there to fight off the wolves, hungry for more information.

Chapter 13

10.30am Tuesday 17th December

Jane Campbell had been thinking about the development in the case ever since she'd watched the ten o'clock news the previous evening. It scared her to think that two people had now been targeted.

Wanting to do something positive, she decided that it was now a suitable time for all the bookshop employees to come together and lay flowers at the door of Ashton's. She knew the general public had been doing so because she'd seen images of the memorial behind reporters who had attended the scene.

She understood as well as anyone that it was difficult for Ashton's employees to return to the shop knowing what had taken place there, but she felt it was the right thing to do. Jane was under no illusion that it would make any difference to Dennis, but she wanted them all to show solidarity with his family.

In turn she called each of the people who had been working at the shop. Her conversation with most was brief and professional. She wasn't a woman who believed it was right or proper to show your feelings publicly. And she had not been especially close to Dennis but, nonetheless, his murder was upsetting and disturbing.

After having spoken to the others, Jane dialled Steven Fisher's number.

'Hello?' He sounded as if he'd just woken up.

'Steven, it's Jane.' Her words were clipped. She couldn't abide laziness. *How on earth could he still be asleep at this time in the morning?*

'Jane, hi.' He yawned.

'I hope you're well.' Her mother had taught her that manners were everything.

'Yes, can't complain.'

'Good, well, I've been thinking, and I think it would be a good idea if everyone who worked at Ashton's arranged for a wreath to be laid at the bookshop, in memory of Dennis. I've spoken to everyone else and they are all on board. I wanted to get your approval and donation before I went ahead and ordered it.'

There was a brief silence.

'Steven?' She wondered if the line had cut out.

'Yeah, sorry, just waking up,' he crackled.

'I see, well, yes, would you be interested in contributing?'

'Sure, why not.'

'Good, that's excellent. We think that it should be simple. You know, white flowers, greenery, that sort of thing.'

'It won't last long in this weather. Maybe something other than flowers might work better.'

Jane did not appreciate anyone interfering with her plans, even if they did have a valid point. 'I see. What would you suggest?' She gripped the phone.

'Dunno. Not really my sort of thing.'

'Well, if you think flowers are a mistake, then it would be a wise idea if you had an alternative you could suggest.'

'Do whatever, Jane.' Steven sighed deeply. 'It was just a passing comment.'

'I shall give it some thought,' Jane said, knowing that she wouldn't.

'Okay.'

'Have you seen the latest reports on the case?'

'What do you mean?'

'The second murder.' Jane could feel the excitement creeping into her voice.

'Oh, you mean that woman?' There was no thrill in Steven's voice.

'Yes. Terrible.' Jane was disappointed he seemed so uninterested.

'Sure. Not a nice way to go.'

'Certainly not!'

'Seems like the police are going around in circles, though,' he drawled.

'Why do you say that?'

'Dunno. Just they don't seem to be getting very far, do they?'

'I don't suppose we are meant to know how the investigation is going. Not the sort of thing they are likely to share.'

'Guess not.'

'Did you speak to them?'

'Yeah I did. Had an interview at the station.'

'Oh?' This piqued her interest. 'They spoke to me at my house.' There was a touch of smugness in her voice but, in reality, she would have loved to go to the police station. It would have been exciting.

'Yeah, I think I was last on their list or something and they've had their hands full with this woman, I suppose. No time for house calls now they have a double murder to investigate.'

'Yes indeed. Anyway, I will arrange something…' That thing being a floral wreath; she hoped he understood her meaning. 'For the memorial, and then get in touch to arrange a time.'

'A time for what?' Steven sat up in bed, perplexed.

'For us all to go to the bookshop and lay it.'

'Oh. I thought you just wanted us to give some money towards it.'

'Well I do, but we should be there to lay it don't you think?'

'Suppose. If you think that's the right thing to do.'

'I do.'

'I'll be in touch when everything is in place.'

'Right.' Steven stifled a groan.

'Have a good day.' Jane hung up and immediately dialled the number of a local florist and ordered a large wreath, despite the fact the weather report had warned of more snow.

***

In Balsham, Francesca was hoping to make plans for Christmas. She hadn't broached the subject with Veronica but with it only being eight days away she was beginning to worry.

Francesca had no intention of letting her sister spend Christmas day on her own, but she also wanted to be back with her husband. Her daughter was meant to be visiting from New Zealand and her flight was due on December the twenty-second.

She and her daughter, Natalie, were complete opposites. Natalie was a free spirit who had flown the nest at her earliest opportunity. She was an artist who had fallen in love with a Kiwi and had moved back to his home country to build a life with him. There was no animosity between mother and daughter, but they would never really understand one another.

Francesca was sad that her only child lived on the other side of the world and that she had little idea about what her life in New Zealand was like. But she did like Leo and could sleep easy knowing that he was taking good care of her daughter.

Natalie had not been back to Britain for nearly two years and this was the first time she would see her mother since her last visit. Francesca had been looking forward to her arrival ever since the trip had been planned in June. But now the day was growing ever closer Francesca was worried her time spent with her daughter was in danger of being cut short.

Veronica was in the sitting room looking blankly at the television screen, on which a breakfast morning show was discussing if the religious meaning of Christmas was still relevant. Francesca, as a Christian, was offended by this. She took it upon herself to switch the television off and start a conversation about what the next few weeks held in store for her sister.

'Here you are.' Francesca put a cup of tea down on the table next to where her sister was sitting. 'I put two sugars in. You need to keep your energy up. I noticed you didn't have any breakfast this morning again.' Veronica stared at the mug but didn't pick it up. 'Anyway,' Francesca continued, 'I know this is difficult, but I think we need to have a talk about next week.'

'Next week?' Veronica was distant.

'Yes, it's Christmas.'

'Not for me it isn't.' She hung her head. 'Dennis always used to buy the tree. There won't be one this year.' She looked at the space in the living room where a tree should have been standing proudly with twinkling lights.

'I know it is the last thing you want to think about but I need to know what I'm doing.' Francesca sat on the sofa next to her sister and rested her hand on her knee. Veronica was still in her dressing gown. 'Natalie is coming over, remember I told you? She lands on the twenty-second and I really don't want to miss spending as much time with her as possible.'

'Natalie? Oh yes.' Veronica had been a good aunt to Natalie when she was young, but as soon as she grew up and left the country the relationship had ended. It wasn't that Veronica was a mean woman, she was just forgetful. Natalie was far away and for Veronica out of sight was out of mind.

'Well, I want to know where you would like to be. I think it would be wise if you came back to Yoxter for a while. What do you think?' Since offending Veronica with her suspicions about Andrew, Francesca had consciously decided to be softer with her sister. 'We could meet Natalie at Heathrow on the twenty-second and travel back with her to Somerset. I think it will do you good to get away from this place for a while.'

'You want me to leave this house?' Veronica looked appalled.

'Just for a little while. Come back home with me. We'll take good care of you. I've spoken to Doug and he thinks it is a good idea.'

'Doug wants me to come and stay?'

'Of course. You're his family too.' Francesca was lying about Doug. She hadn't run the idea past her husband at all, but she knew she didn't need to. She wore the trousers; Doug always allowed his wife to make the decisions and fell into line with them.

'But you want to spend time with Natalie. I'd just be in the way.'

'No, you wouldn't,' she lied. 'I'm not going to leave you here alone.'

'But I won't be any fun. I can't pretend to be jolly. I don't want to eat turkey or open presents. It's just not right. Not without my Dennis. And I'm worried sick about Andrew. How can you expect me to celebrate?' A large tear streamed down Veronica's plump and pale face.

'No one expects you to want to celebrate. If you want, you don't even have to join us for Christmas lunch, but I won't leave you here alone and I can't stay. I just can't. I've not seen Natalie for two years.' Francesca felt flustered by the stress of it all.

'Okay,' she finally agreed, seeing the despair on her sister's face. 'I'll come with you. You're right. There is no point staying here on my own. It won't do me any good.'

'That's that then.' Francesca clapped her hands together with relief and stood up. 'Natalie can sleep on the sofa and you can have her room. I'll tell Doug to have everything ready. He can meet us at Heathrow and drive us all back. Don't you worry about a thing.' She picked up the now cold and untouched cup of tea and took it into the kitchen, leaving Veronica alone. She felt relieved that they had cleared up one matter but knew there was another pressing subject she still needed to address.

Before too long, she would have to speak to her sister about Dennis's funeral but that could wait for another day. They all needed to take things one step at a time and, as Francesca filled the sink with hot water and washing up liquid, she looked out of the window over the garden. Snow was beginning to fall again.

***

Elly Hale sat at her desk going through the reports on the phone calls that the Crimestoppers helpline and the station had received since the press conference. They had received a lot of bogus calls from people who were either lonely, mad or bored. But when she came across a statement from a group of students who had been out partying late, she felt a glimmer of hope.

It seemed a young woman had seen a person hanging around outside the back of Ashton's Bookshop on the night of Dennis Wade's murder. The woman claimed that, at first, she thought the person might be homeless, but when she spotted the figure peering in through a window she realised they were watching the premises. At the time, she said, she hadn't given it much thought as a blizzard was blowing and she and her friends were late for a party at one of the halls of residence. When the witness had been asked what time this took place she said she thought it was around eight o'clock in the evening. She had described the figure as tall and wearing a dark hooded coat or jacket. The description was strikingly similar to the image the police had found on CCTV. Elly scribbled down the contact details of the witness and returned to trawling through the rest of the recorded calls.

Unlike the city centre of Cambridge, Ickleton had practically no CCTV so even if the killer had been scoping out New Barn there would be no evidence.

When Elly knocked on Barrett's door to give him an update a thought occurred to her.

'Sir?' She let herself in, conscious that he hadn't given any verbal permission.

'Yes?' Barrett was hunched over his computer.

'We have an eye-witness report claiming they saw someone acting suspiciously outside Ashton's Bookshop on the night of Mr Wade's murder. She hadn't brought over the transcript of the recorded conversation for her superior to look at. 'I've made a note of the witness's telephone number and home address.'

'Good.' He slid the paperwork back to her and continued tapping on his keyboard expecting her to leave. But when she didn't, he finally looked up. 'What is it?'

'I've been thinking.' Elly bit her lip for a moment. 'It might be a good idea to look back over CCTV footage further back than the night of the murder. If, as we believe, the killer has been following his victims for some time, in order to familiarise themselves with their routines, then it is possible that there may be more footage of our suspect. Perhaps even footage that might give us a better look at our perpetrator.' Elly held her breath waiting to hear what her boss thought about her suggestion.

'Excellent idea. Get onto the CCTV control room and ask them to go through footage over the last three months.'

'Yes, sir!' Elly was extremely pleased that her idea had been welcomed.

'If they need more manpower to trawl through the footage, then you can go over there, and take Singh with you.'

Suddenly Elly wasn't so thrilled.

'Good work, Hale.' Barrett stopped typing for a moment. 'Anything useful on the Matlock murder?'

'Not yet. The weather hasn't helped. Most people are tucked up in their homes, not walking around the streets. It's going to be difficult to find a witness who saw anything in Ickleton.'

'Difficult yes.' Barrett stopped and put his long bony finger in the air. 'But not impossible. Keep digging.'

'Shall I stay here and continue doing that or do you want me to go with Singh down to the control room?' Behind her back Elly crossed her fingers.

'Do I have to make every decision myself? Show some initiative.' Barrett waved her away and Elly returned to the incident room knowing full well she had no intention of spending the next few days cooped up in the dingy control room. Singh, unbeknownst to him, had drawn the short straw.

Palmer was sitting at his desk, with a serious expression carved onto his face. Elly spotted him from the other side of the room and decided to share the development with him before delivering the bad news to Singh.

'What's up?' She sat on the edge of his desk, her pencil skirt tight on her thighs as she crossed her legs.

Palmer straightened in his seat, doing his best to ignore her curves. 'I've just got off the phone to the French police. It seems Andrew Wade is still nowhere to be seen. An APB has been sent out to all the hospitals and businesses in the local area, where he was last seen, but no one has reported any sightings.'

'You think he's guilty?' Elly cocked her head, letting her poker-straight espresso-coloured hair fall down over one of her shoulders.

'No, I don't. But I think the sooner we bring him in the sooner we can dismiss him from this enquiry.'

'He does have a motive,' Elly said thoughtfully.

'For Dennis Wade, yes, but Matlock? I don't think so.' Palmer shook his head to emphasise the point while trying to dismiss the idea that Elly might be deliberately flirting with him.

'Still nothing to link the victims?' She tucked her hair behind her ear.

'No,' Palmer grunted. 'Not a sodding thing.'

Chapter 14

Veronica sat listening to Francesca talk about her memories of Natalie as a small child. Natalie, unlike Andrew, had been popular and liked. She had been a pretty child with blonde hair, which her mother often used to put up in a French plait. She wasn't exactly academic, but she was clever, and her artistic flair blossomed early. Where her artistic ability came from no one quite knew. Neither Doug nor Francesca could ever be accused of having such talents. Doug had been a primary school science teacher and Francesca used to work in a doctor's surgery on reception. The position suited her well. She was organised, efficient and enjoyed the small amount of power the role gave her.

As Veronica zoned out of the monologue her sister was conducting, she found herself thinking back to Andrew's childhood and the happy times she had spent with her son and husband.

Often, during the summer, the three of them would rent a mobile caravan on the Norfolk coast. The week would be spent crabbing off Cromer pier and exploring the quaint villages dotted around the rolling countryside. Dennis never did like eating crab, but he enjoyed catching the crustaceans and then letting them go again.

The weather, as is always the case in England, couldn't be relied upon but it never stopped them from enjoying themselves. During the evening Veronica and Andrew would play cards, while Dennis read a book. Andrew, she now realised, had probably been lonely without a sibling and Veronica found herself wondering why they never had more children. It hadn't been something she and Dennis ever discussed. Their sex life had declined rapidly after Andrew was born and Veronica had never broached the subject with her husband for fear of looking needy or insecure. She had been brought up to bury her feelings, something that came far more naturally to her sister than it ever had done to Veronica.

As Francesca continued to waffle on about what a perfect daughter she had raised, Veronica found herself wondering why Natalie had emigrated to the other side of the world. Andrew, for all his faults, had never gone far from home. But now he was somewhere in France, alone, on the run from the police. The thought made her heart bleed and she wondered how much more pain she could take. What had she done to deserve this? Veronica had never been a great believer in karma but suddenly she entertained the idea that perhaps she was being punished for something.

She found herself trapped within her own mind unable to escape. The walls of the house began to feel as if they were closing in and her heart started beating furiously in her chest, threatening to break through her ribs.

Finally, Francesca stopped talking, realising something was wrong.

'Veronica?' She placed her hand on her sister's shoulder, but Veronica didn't appear to hear. 'Are you all right?'

Veronica couldn't respond. She was frozen to the spot, unable to move, unable to even blink.

'What is it?' Francesca gently shook her sister desperate for a response.

'Cromer.'

'Cromer?'

'I want to go back to Cromer.'

Francesca nodded not understanding what on earth her sister was talking about.

'Where are my cards?' Veronica stood, almost knocking her sister over. 'I need to find my cards.'

Francesca watched as her sister moved around the living room opening every drawer, frantically searching.

'What cards?'

'For snap. We need them for snap.'

'Snap?' Francesca was completely lost, and she worried that Veronica was losing her mind, but before she could say anything the phone rang.

Leaving Veronica still frantically searching, she went into the small hallway and answered the phone.

'Wade residence.' The fact that she sounded like Hyacinth Bucket, from *Keeping Up Appearances*, was entirely lost on her but not on Palmer.

'DI Palmer.'

'Inspector. It's Francesca Woodcock. How can I help you?'

'We'd like to come over and speak to Mrs Wade, please. Is now a good time?'

Francesca stared through the doorway at Veronica who had collapsed in a heap on the sofa and was sobbing.

'I'll have her ready for you.' She sighed, wanting to hang up and attend to her sister.

'Thank you. See you in twenty minutes,' he said before ending the call.

Veronica was still huddled in a ball crying. She barely noticed when Francesca came back into the room.

'DI Palmer is on his way. He wants to talk to you.' Francesca stood over her sister unable to comfort her. 'Let's get you cleaned up. We can't have the inspector seeing you in this state.'

Francesca had seen Veronica distraught over the last few days but what she witnessed that afternoon was something entirely different. Struggling to know what to do to help calm her, Francesca decided that the only thing to do was to give her sister a large measure of whisky. Much to her surprise and relief it seemed to do the trick; so, when Palmer arrived, fifteen minutes later, Veronica was in a much more suitable state.

'Mrs Wade.' The DI extended his hand and shook Veronica's warmly. 'Thank you for agreeing to see us at such short notice.'

Elly, who stood next to Palmer, offered a small awkward smile. She wondered if she'd ever get used to dealing with relatives of murder victims. In one way she hoped she wouldn't.

Veronica, who stayed mute, showed them into the kitchen where Francesca was preparing a pot of tea.

'Your garden looks very pretty in the snow,' Elly commented while looking through the window as large light flakes tumbled down from the sky.

'Dennis was the gardener,' Veronica said numbly.

'Tea anyone?' Francesca smiled brightly, placing the teapot down on the table.

'I am sorry to do this, but I need to talk to you about your son,' Palmer said as he accepted the floral cup and saucer foisted upon him.

Francesca tutted as she poured tea into his cup.

'Have you found him?' The hope in Veronica's eyes was heartbreaking.

'No, I'm afraid not.'

'Well what then?' Francesca was nothing if not to the point.

'I need to ask you about an argument Andrew had with his father in November.'

Hearing those words, Veronica's heart sank. 'You mean about the bail money?'

'Yes.' He did not enjoy the fact he was inflicting more pain on an already broken woman. 'Did you know that your husband had refused to give Andrew money?'

'No.' Veronica felt foolish admitting it. 'But the only reason he would have kept it from me would have been to protect me. He knew how upset I got whenever Andrew got into trouble.'

'Why do you think your husband refused on that occasion?'

'This is not easy to admit.' Veronica hung her head and let out a small sigh. 'But Dennis had given up on Andrew.'

Elly chewed the inside of her cheek feeling like she was in the audience of *The Jeremy Kyle Show*.

'We have helped Andrew financially time and time again. He always promises that it will be the last time... until we receive another call. It has been never-ending. His father was so disappointed. It pained him that his son was a drug addict and a criminal. I suppose he'd just had enough.' She paused, considering something for a moment. 'I have to ask, why was Andrew arrested in November?' She wasn't sure she really wanted to hear the answer.

'He was found with herbal cannabis.'

Francesca kissed her teeth and shook her head, completely unsurprised by the revelation. 'That boy,' she muttered to herself.

Veronica glared at her sister. 'He is your family too.' She gently reminded her.

Francesca stiffened in her seat.

'I have to tell you that we believe Andrew has been in a car crash.' Palmer said it as softly as he could, but it made no difference. The impact of the words was still there.

'A crash?' Veronica looked horrified.

'The French police found his car on the side of a motorway. It had collided into a tree. There was no sign of Andrew but we do believe he might be injured.'

For the first time since the whole affair had begun, Francesca found herself worried about Andrew. It was not a feeling she was familiar with and she wasn't sure how to cope with it, especially when Veronica turned to her looking terrified.

'He's injured?' Her voice shook.

'We doubt it is very serious.' Elly tried to soothe Veronica. 'But we do think it would be best if he handed himself in.'

'The French police are releasing a picture of Andrew to the news channels over there, in the hope that someone might have seen him.'

This was the final straw for Veronica. 'I'm sorry,' she said, as she stood up, knocking over and breaking the bone china cup, 'I can't do this.'

Francesca sprang into action and immediately started to mop up the tepid tea that was threatening to pool off the pine table onto the vinyl tiles below. 'She's very upset,' she apologised as her sister disappeared out of the kitchen. They heard the sound of her footsteps on the stairs. 'It's an extremely difficult time. And what with it being Christmas.'

Palmer always wondered why people said that. There was never a good time for anyone to die, was there? Would it have been more convenient if someone had strung Dennis up in the middle of July? Perhaps March was a better time to learn that your husband had been murdered.

'I am terribly sorry.' He stood, holding onto his tie and making sure it didn't fall into the puddle of tea that was creeping closer to him. 'We'll leave you in peace.'

'Inspector, now that my sister is out of the room, please tell me, how badly do you think Andrew is injured?'

'We can't know for sure. His car obviously hit the tree at some speed.'

'But if he was really hurt, I'm sure he would have taken himself to hospital,' Elly interrupted, wanting to be encouraging. 'It's probably just a scratch.'

Francesca stopped wiping the table and stared at the sergeant. 'Do you have children?' She asked in an accusatory tone.

'No, I don't.' Elly blushed.

'Then you will never know the pain a mother feels for her child.'

'Thank you again for the tea,' Palmer cut in, wanting to protect his colleague from a verbal bashing. He guided Elly out of the house leaving Francesca scowling.

'Wow. She's a piece of work,' Elly said once they were outside.

'She's a fire-cracker.' Palmer smirked.

'It's good to know that Mrs Wade has someone there for her, though.' She reached over and brushed a snowflake off Palmer's shoulder. The pair looked at each other for a moment and said nothing. There was something between them, and Palmer could feel it growing.

'Right.' He led the way back to the car, crunching through the newly fallen snow. 'Back to the station.'

Elly followed behind, stepping in his footprints, knowing that she had feelings for this man and that he was married. She wasn't a homewrecker but spending so much time together was making it difficult to ignore the attraction she felt towards him. She suspected that he felt it too and that only made the situation worse.

As they got into the car, grateful to be out of the bitter cold, Palmer's mobile phone began to ring. Barrett's name was on the screen. Pulling off his gloves he fumbled in a hurry trying to answer it in time. 'Sir?'

'We've got a situation. I need you and Hale back here now. We've had reports from the French authorities that Andrew Wade is staying in a hotel in Vaas, north of Tours. They are on their way there now.'

When Elly and Palmer returned to the station, they were surprised to find Tilly Edgely in reception. She looked like she hadn't slept for a week. Her hair was a mess, she wore loose-fitting clothes that did nothing for her figure and her once bright eyes were sunken in her face.

'Miss Edgely,' Palmer greeted her warmly.

'I just wanted to find out what's going on.' She chewed the sleeve of her jumper nervously while Elly and Palmer shared a concerned look.

'I really can't disclose details of an on-going case.' He was half apologetic.

'But, but...' Tilly's hands shook and her eyes pleaded.

'Why don't you come with me.' Elly put her arm around Tilly's broad shoulders, noticing how tall she was, and led her away from the people staring in reception. Palmer nodded gratefully and headed up the stairs.

'We really can't tell you much, I'm afraid,' Elly said, guiding Tilly towards a blue nylon armchair.

'Are they going to get me?' She looked frightened and searched Elly's face for comfort and answers.

'Who?' Elly asked softly.

'The killer. Are they going to come after me too?'

'Why would you think that?' She did little to disguise her shock.

'Two people now. Two.' Tilly counted on her fingers. 'Maybe I'm next.'

'Listen.' Elly reached over and put her hand on Tilly's knee to stop it shaking. 'We have no reason to believe you are in any danger, Miss Edgely. We're doing everything we can to catch the person responsible.'

'I don't want to end up like Dennis,' she sobbed. 'I don't want to die alone in the dark.' She covered her eyes with the palms of her hands, trying to escape the visual memories that swirled around her head.

'Has something happened that has led you to think you are a target?'

'Two people.' Tilly counted on her fingers again, her childlike vulnerability shining through.

'It's perfectly normal to be upset. You saw a horrible thing.' Elly wished she was upstairs where the action was going on, rather than dealing with an emotionally fragile witness who was clearly on the cusp of nervous breakdown.

'The news said it's a serial killer,' Tilly said in a whisper. 'They could be after any of us.'

'It's true we are working on the assumption that the same killer is responsible for both murders.' Elly couldn't deny that. 'But, at the moment, there is no reason for you to think you're in any danger.'

'We're all in danger,' she insisted.

Elly didn't know what to say. She felt that Tilly would be better off having this conversation with a psychiatrist.

'Do you have any plans for Christmas?' She decided the only course of action was to change the subject.

'I can't leave. You won't let me leave.'

'Are you spending it with your family?' Elly was exasperated.

'They're in Dorset. You told me I have to stay in Cambridge.' Large tears rolled down her gaunt cheeks.

'Stay here a moment, I'll be right back.' The sergeant left the room closing the door behind her and leaning on it for a moment to compose herself. The intensity in the room had been a lot for her to handle. Returning to reception she asked the officer behind the desk to put a call in to Barrett's office.

'What?' Barrett barked down the line, having been interrupted by the call.

'Sir, I'm downstairs with Tilly Edgely. She's in a very bad way. I was wondering if perhaps it would be okay for me to tell her she can return home to Dorset for Christmas. What do you think?' Elly held her breath.

'Yes, yes. Fine. She's not a suspect.' Barrett banged the phone down ending the conversation.

When Elly returned to tell Tilly the good news, she found the young woman huddling in the corner of the room rubbing her temples with her fingers.

'I've just spoke to DCI Barrett who says you don't have to stay in Cambridge. Now you can go home to your family. That'll be nice, won't it.' Elly smiled, pleased that she had been able to do something to help Tilly.

'But I have to stay and help.' Tilly's eyes were wide and staring. 'I need to find his glasses.'

'Whose glasses?' Elly asked.

'Mr Wade's. He can't see without them.'

Chapter 15

After collecting the white wreath of lilies from the florist, Jane made her way into the centre of Cambridge on the bus. The snow had temporarily stopped falling and the city looked serene.

Hopping off the bus outside John Lewis, Jane walked slowly holding the large flower display, enjoying the looks of interest she received from the people who were Christmas shopping. In the distance she could hear the faint sound of a choir singing carols in the Market Square.

Before she'd left the house, Jane had contacted her colleagues and requested that they met her outside the shop. She wanted them all to collectively lay the wreath. Marcus, Steven and Tilly had agreed to join her. The others either had plans or she hadn't been able to get in touch with them.

As Jane turned onto the Market Square the singing grew louder. Gathered outside the front of the Great St Mary's Church stood a choir, wrapped up in their scarves, hats and gloves, singing *Carol of the Bells*. The music was carried around the walls of the buildings by the gentle breeze.

Realising she was running late, Jane quickened her pace as she turned onto Trinity Street. She was only five minutes late, but she had always prided herself on being punctual.

When she turned the corner on the cobbled street, she saw Marcus, Tilly and Steven all huddled in front of the small memorial in front of the bookshop. More snow had fallen since the flowers, candles and tokens had been laid and the memorial looked rather pathetic. Jane felt instantly gratified that she had done the right thing by arranging the wreath.

'Hello,' Jane announced her arrival.

'You're late.' Marcus was not pleased about this. He checked his watch.

'I apologise. The florist had a problem with their till.'

'Let's get on with it shall we?' Marcus was not enjoying standing in the cold.

'It's lovely,' Tilly said in a mousey voice and pointed to the wreath.

'Thank you.' Jane admired the floral display as if she herself had constructed it.

Steven puffed on a rolled-up cigarette and hugged himself for warmth.

Jane handed the wreath to Tilly for a moment before bending down to brush away some of the snow from the other gifts with a leather-gloved hand.

'Should one of us say a few words?' Marcus asked.

'It's not his funeral,' Steven pointed out, perhaps hoping to avoid any unnecessary morbid interaction.

'How odd,' Jane said, still hunched down clearing snow away.

'What is?' Tilly took a step back.

'Look.' She pointed at a small cardboard box that was among the other items left by mourners.

The others gathered around her and peered down at the box. On the top of it in black letters were the words *Now You See Me…*

'That is strange.' Marcus curled his lip slightly and pulled his camelhair coat tighter around his waist.

'What's in it?' Steven asked.

'I don't know. Do you think we should open it?' It was in Jane's nature to be inquisitive but there was something about the box that made her feel uneasy.

'No.' Tilly put even more distance between herself and the box. 'We shouldn't touch it. It's not for us. Leave it alone.'

'Don't be so dramatic, darling.' Marcus rolled his eyes. 'It's not a bomb!'

'How do you know?' Tilly protested.

Again, Marcus rolled his eyes but refused to answer the question.

'I think open it.' Steven stubbed his cigarette out on a wall and flicked the butt away.

'It does look out of place.' Jane picked up the box carefully.

'Either open it or don't, but please let's get on with it. It's awfully chilly.' Marcus rubbed his hands together for effect.

Jane stood and turned to face the other three before carefully removing the top of the cardboard box. She peered inside, a puzzled look on her face.

'What is it?' Tilly was terrified of what the answer might be.

'How strange.' Jane looked up to see the questioning expressions on the three faces.

'Well?' Marcus had always been impatient.

'It's a pair of glasses.' Carefully Jane removed them from the box.

'They look familiar.' Marcus took them in his hands and inspected them.

'That's because they are.' Tilly had a wild grin on her face. 'They're Dennis's glasses.' She dropped the wreath onto the ground and clapped her hands together with glee before letting out a maniacal laugh.

Jane, who was horrified to see that the wreath had been damaged and that some of the lily heads had broken off, bent down to retrieve and fix the floral offering she had been so determined to arrange.

'Bit odd.' Steven indicated to the glasses as he began to roll another cigarette.

'They were missing.' Tilly's eyes were glinting with joy. 'He didn't have them on when I found him.' The frantic words fell from her mouth. 'I was so worried. I wanted to find them. It wasn't right that he didn't have his glasses. He always wore his glasses, didn't he?' She turned to Steven, a pleading look on her face.

'Sure. Yeah.' Steven noticed how unhinged she looked.

'But he's got them back now. It's all okay. Now he can see again and now I can go home.' She turned and walked off into the wintery distance leaving three people staring after her.

'She's quite mad,' Marcus said, still holding onto the glasses.

'Poor girl.' Jane shook her head. 'She's been badly affected by this.'

'Do you know what she meant when she said that the glasses had been missing?' Marcus took the box from Jane and placed the glasses back inside.

'No idea.' Jane shrugged.

'Well, if she's telling the truth and Dennis's glasses have been missing, they certainly aren't now. Someone brought them back.' His mind was beginning to piece together what the discovery meant.

'Who?' Steven asked.

'I think we should call the police.' Marcus turned back to face the shop and gently placed the box down in the place they had found it.

'You think it might be evidence?' Jane was still holding the damaged wreath.

'Looks that way don't you think?' he said gravely.

'Grim.' Steven lit his cigarette. 'Shall we lay this thing then, or not?' He pointed to the floral arrangement.

'Let's get it over and done with,' Marcus encouraged.

'Very well.' Jane approached the memorial and placed the slightly dishevelled wreath down. 'Rest in peace,' she said quietly before stepping back.

'It was a nice idea of yours.' Steven patted her shoulder.

'It was right that we did something,' Marcus agreed, removing his mobile phone from his coat pocket. 'But now I think we need to call the police.'

'Do we all have to hang around then?' Steven enquired.

'Unfortunately, I suspect so.' He sighed while searching for the number of Parkside Police Station.

'Shall we call Tilly back?' Jane suggested turning to Steven.

'The police can catch up with her if they need to. Let her go.' He dragged furiously on his cigarette.

The pair listened as Marcus explained to an officer on the end of the line that they had discovered the box containing the glasses.

'They are sending someone now and, yes, we do have to stay for the moment,' he groaned.

'It's too cold to be standing on the street. Let's get a coffee and come back in five minutes,' Jane suggested, wanting to put some distance between herself and the box with the strange message.

'Sounds like a plan to me,' Steven said, while Marcus nodded in agreement.

The three set off in silence, heading towards Bridge Street, passing some of the most beautiful historic university buildings in the city.

'What do you think it meant?' Jane was the first to break the silence.

'What did what mean?' Marcus walked with his head down looking at all the footprints in the snow.

'*Now You See Me…* What do you think it meant?'

'It is rather cryptic.'

'It is, isn't it,' Steven said thoughtfully.

***

'I know, sir, get onto CCTV.' Singh closed the door to Barrett's office.

'He's playing with us, Joe.' Barrett stood behind his desk looking out over Parker's Piece. Families had come out to play in the new snow. Children built snowmen and threw snowballs while dogs romped around them.

'The schools broke up yesterday,' Palmer told him, also watching the people below as the phone began to ring.

'Barrett,' he snatched the phone up quickly. There was a long silence while the person on the other end of the phone delivered information. 'Very well, thank you for the update.'

Palmer raised an eyebrow.

'They've got Andrew Wade. Picked him up a few hours ago.'

'Right.' This news didn't excite Palmer. He was now more convinced than ever that Andrew had nothing to do with the murders. 'No way he could have left the glasses there, though, is there.'

'We don't know how long they've been there,' Barrett said sitting down. He wasn't ready to let his suspect entirely off the hook just yet. 'He lied about the last time he had contact with his father and then he left the country, while on bail. He knows something.'

'Or he's just an idiot,' Palmer said flatly.

'The box with the glasses has been sent over to forensics. Let's see if they come up with anything. In the meantime, I want you to speak to Shane Matlock again. I want to know why he was paying the mortgage on a house he wasn't living in, especially when he has a pregnant girlfriend to support. Tell him to come to the station.'

'I will.' Palmer started to move towards the door and then stopped. 'What do you think it meant, the words on the box?'

'Now you see me... now you don't,' Barrett said slowly.

'Do you think the message is for us?'

'Perhaps.'

'We should send a car over to Ickleton to see if anything has been left at the scene there.'

'I'll leave that to you. Get Hale onto it.'

'Yes, sir.' Palmer closed the door to the office and walked purposefully over to his desk, summoning Elly with a wave of his hand as he did so. 'Send a car over to New Barn to check the scene for anything that might have been left there, please. I'm going to request Shane Matlock comes in and talks to us. You can sit in on the interview.'

Palmer was being much more formal with Elly than usual. It unnerved her. 'Will do.'

'Oh, and they've apprehended Andrew Wade in France.' Palmer sat typing at his desk without looking up.

'Well that's good news.' Elly ran some lip balm over her mouth, using her finger to apply it. 'Once he's been questioned then we can concentrate on finding the person responsible.'

Palmer said nothing in response so, with a sigh, Elly left to go arrange for officers to search the crime scene in Ickleton.

He stopped typing and sat back in his chair, watching Elly walk away. Because of the method the killer had used on Dennis and Wendy, Palmer knew the person responsible was not only smart but also extremely dangerous. And now they were playing games. This gave the police a glimmer of light. When a psychopath started showing off they often got sloppy. Palmer found himself praying that the murderer would slip up sooner rather than later and hoped there would be no more deaths in the meantime.

Half an hour later, after a phone call with Shane Matlock, Barrett approached Palmer.

'They are putting Andrew Wade on the next flight back to Stansted,' Barrett informed him. 'We'll be there to greet him when he lands tomorrow morning.'

'Shane Matlock has agreed to come in and talk to us. He will be here in an hour.' Palmer looked at the clock on the wall seeing that it was already nearly six o'clock in the evening.

'Good. Time for something to eat then,' Barrett suggested realising he hadn't had any lunch.

'Fancy a kebab from Mill Road?'

'Yes. Let's do that.' Barrett went into his office to retrieve his coat before returning to Palmer's desk. 'Let's go.'

Palmer stood up and wrapped a bright red scarf, which had been a present from his son, around his neck.

The two men stepped out of the station and into the cold stillness. Above them the naked tree branches were heavy with snow and the moon shone low in the sky like a beacon.

'Do you have any plans on Christmas day?' Palmer asked, knowing full well that it was possible they would be spending it at the station investigating the murders.

'My sister invited me to stay but I can't stand her husband, so I refused the invitation.'

'Ah yes, the trouble with in-laws.' Palmer grinned. 'Sally was worried you didn't have any plans,' he continued, referring to his wife, 'so she asked me to invite you to spend the day with us.'

'Really?' Barrett was not often taken by surprise.

'Yes. We've got a turkey big enough to feed an army. You're more than welcome.'

'That is a very generous offer,' Barrett said, choking down emotion.

'Obviously if the case is still on-going…' Palmer didn't finish the sentence.

'Obviously,' Barrett agreed as they approached the kebab shop.

***

An hour later they were back at the station and in an interview room with Shane Matlock, who sat nervously in a chair opposite the two inspectors.

'Thank you for agreeing to come in.' Palmer undid the top button on his shirt and loosened his tie. 'We just have a few more questions.'

'We've been looking into Wendy Matlock's finances,' Barrett began. 'It appears that you still pay a large proportion of the mortgage on New Barn. Is that correct?'

'Yes.' Shane looked sheepish.

'Can you tell us why?'

'Wendy and I didn't split up because we stopped loving each other. We just wanted different things. I knew she couldn't afford it on her own, so I carried on making payments. I didn't want her to lose the house as well as me. She didn't deserve that.'

'Very noble,' Barrett said with a hint of sarcasm.

'Does your girlfriend know you are still helping your wife out financially?' Palmer rested his hands on the desk.

'Well, no,' he admitted.

'Why not?'

'It would upset her.'

'But now that Wendy Matlock is dead that problem no longer exists, does it?' Barrett folded his arms.

'No, I suppose not.'

'Tell us again about the last time you saw your wife?' Palmer asked.

'Like I said, I saw her a few weeks ago when I went over to the house to collect some post.' Shane shrugged.

'We understand you defaulted on your last two mortgage payments.' Barrett fixed Shane with a stare.

'That's none of your business.' Shane sat forward angrily.

'I'll think you'll find it is, Mr Matlock,' Barrett replied with a smile. 'This is a murder investigation and we are looking for a motive.'

'Why did you default?' Palmer was keen to take a softer approach.

Shane put his head in his hands and let out a long sigh. 'Business hasn't been great lately. It was killing me paying the mortgage and the rent for my place in Royston. Gemma wanted to stop working when she found out she was pregnant. She said she didn't want to be a working mother. I agreed it would be nice for her to be a stay-at-home mum, but I didn't expect her to hand her notice in to the salon as early as she did. I hadn't had a chance to discuss everything with Wendy.'

'We found letters from the mortgage company demanding payment at the barn.'

'That's why I went to see her. She wanted to know what was going on,' Shane admitted. 'I told her I couldn't afford to keep paying for the barn. I suggested she took in a lodger to help with the cost. There's a big spare room. I also thought it might be nice for her to have some company.' He sounded genuine.

'Did she advertise for a lodger, do you know?' Palmer asked.

'I don't know if she did, but she said she'd think about it. She didn't want to lose the house.' Shane looked sorrowful.

'I don't suppose she did,' Barrett said dryly.

'Does Gemma know you were still paying for the barn?'

'No.' Shane hung his head. 'She wouldn't have liked it, especially with the baby on the way.'

'Have you ever met a Dennis Wade?' Barrett changed tack.

'The dead guy?' Shane looked up.

'The first murder victim,' Barrett corrected.

'No, never met the fella.'

'Do you know if your wife knew Mr Wade at all?'

'Not as far as I know.' Shane ran his hand through his thinning short brown hair.

'We understand that you are the benefactor in Mrs Matlock's will.' Barrett moved the conversation again.

'Yes I am. I suppose she never got round to changing it. She didn't have a great fortune, though, if that's what you're getting at.'

'Had you not discussed divorce, given that you are now living with another woman and expecting a child?' Palmer inquired.

'It did come up,' Shane admitted, 'when I went to see her last time.'

'How did she react?' Barrett pressed.

'I don't think it came as a shock. We were both kind of sad, though. It meant the real end.'

'But neither of you had started the divorce proceedings?'

'No.'

'Why not?'

'It wasn't like there was a huge rush.'

'You say that, Mr Matlock, but I noticed an engagement ring on Gemma's finger,' Palmer confessed.

'She is the mother of my child. Hardly surprising that we plan to get married,' Shane said blushing.

'But you can't get married until the divorce comes through.'

'No, but there is no rush. Gem doesn't want to be a pregnant bride so we're going to wait until the baby is born. We haven't set a date.' He squirmed in his chair.

'Weddings are expensive things,' Barrett added.

'I don't like this.' Shane's face filled with anger. 'What exactly are you getting at?'

'Whoever was responsible for Mrs Matlock's murder was able to gain entry to the house without any difficulty.' Barrett's glare was unwavering.

'So that means I killed her?' Shane spat in disbelief.

'Money is a good motive for murder.' Barrett leaned back in his chair.

'How about you stop wasting my time and catch the person responsible for this. I did not kill my ex-wife,' Shane said through gritted teeth.

'Wife, Mr Matlock. Not ex-wife.'

'Be as pedantic as you like but you're wasting your time on me.' Shane stood up. 'And unless you want to arrest me, I think this conversation is done.'

'Thanks for your time.' Palmer stood in a hurry.

'We'll be in touch if we have any more questions,' Barrett said looking at his fingernails.

'Find the person who did this.' Shane turned to face Palmer. 'Please.'

Chapter 16

Barrett and Palmer stood in Stansted Airport by customs waiting for Andrew Wade to be delivered to them. The French police had arranged the flight and were escorting him back to hand him over to the British authorities.

Stansted was busy with Christmas holidaymakers departing and arriving ahead of the big day.

It wasn't a big surprise when the men were told that a lot of the flights were delayed because of the snow. That morning Barrett had watched the news and reports were coming in from across the country about disrupted flights. He'd wondered why the British were always so useless at dealing with the cold weather. It wasn't as if snow was that uncommon, yet every time it hit the country it seemed to come to a standstill. Schools closed, roads shut and airports found themselves in chaos, and this seemed to happen even if there was only a light sprinkling of the cold stuff.

While they waited for the plane to arrive, Barrett received a call from Bob Roland the pathologist.

'Ian.'

Barrett immediately stiffened.

'Bob, any news?'

'No DNA on the box or the glasses, apart from some belonging to the victim.'

'Damn it.'

'I can confirm that there was Rohypnol in Wendy Matlock's system and that the cause of death was asphyxiation.'

'Anything else?'

'We found traces of semen in her vagina.'

'She was raped?' Barrett asked in shock.

'No signs of rape.'

'So consensual.' Barrett pondered this.

'I would say that sexual intercourse took place shortly before her death.'

Palmer watched Barrett's face with fascination and listened carefully to as much of the conversation as he could gather.

'I've run the DNA we retrieved from the sperm through our system. It hasn't come up with a match.'

'I want a swab to be taken from the estranged husband. I don't think he's our man but we need to rule him out,' Barrett said looking at Palmer.

'Righto.'

'I have to go. Speak soon.'

Barrett hung up and crossed his arms, tapping his foot impatiently on the ground.

'Wendy Matlock had sex shortly before her death,' he finally told, Palmer who had already gathered as much from listening to his boss on the phone.

But Palmer wasn't really listening. He was looking up at the arrivals board, watching with interest the updates on the delays. According to the information screen, Andrew's flight should be landing within the next twenty minutes.

Meanwhile the queues at customs were quickly becoming gridlocked. From somewhere near the back of the queue, Barrett and Palmer could hear a passenger losing not only their temper but also the will to live. The voice gradually grew louder and the pitch more offensive. Others in the line, who had been preoccupied with their own frustrations, now turned to see where the commotion was coming from.

Bemused, Palmer watched as airport security fought their way through the crowd towards the fray. From where he stood, he couldn't see the person responsible for all the noise and disruption, but he could hear that a man and a woman were going at it hammer and tongs. She was screaming and he was shouting back. Palmer guessed they might have been a couple who had both come to their wits' end. He imagined a small child, stuck crying between the bellowing adults.

Though they both felt they should insert themselves into the action and put an end to the drama, Barrett and Palmer came to a silent agreement that it would be best if they stayed put and left the issue to airport security. Irate passengers at airports were neither their preference nor their speciality.

Once the dispute between the couple had been dealt with, fellow passengers turned their attention back to their own frustration about waiting in a queue.

Barrett finally breathed a sigh of relief when the arrivals boards notified them that Andrew Wade's flight had landed. Holding his badge up, he carved a path through the human traffic, like Moses through the Red Sea, followed closely by Palmer.

The men made their way to gate number forty-one and waited to escort Andrew Wade to their car and back to the station.

When Wade appeared, handcuffed and flanked by two French police officers, his injuries from the crash were evident. The bridge of his nose was swollen and there were puffy bruises beneath both of his eyes. He also had a deep gash across his forehead.

'Andrew Wade, I am arresting you on suspicion of murder and for absconding while on bail. You do not have to say anything but anything you do say may be used in evidence against you.' As quickly as the French handcuffs had been removed the English pair clicked shut around his wrists.

'You have been in the wars, Andrew,' Palmer said as they walked along the corridor back towards customs. Wade said nothing and hung his head looking like a dejected man. 'Why did you run?' Palmer continued, but still Andrew stayed quiet.

'You'll be assigned a solicitor as soon as we get to the station.' Barrett glared at Palmer, signalling for him to shut up.

Barrett knew that any statement Andrew Wade made before he had been formally charged at the station and given the opportunity to speak to a solicitor would be null and void. Not only that, but Palmer would face a disciplinary hearing for breaking the code of conduct. As far as Barrett was concerned, Andrew wasn't worth taking the risk for.

Pleased to be stepping out of the heaving airport, Barrett led Andrew to the police car and bundled him into the back seat. 'Make yourself comfortable,' he said before slamming the door closed.

By the time they had managed to get off the M11 and made it back to Parkside Police Station it was nearly lunchtime.

Andrew was processed at the front desk and then thrown into a cell. Barrett and Palmer took themselves off for some well-deserved coffee and sandwiches, while they waited for the state solicitor to arrive to represent the suspect.

Once their appetites were satisfied the inspectors turned their attention back to Andrew Wade. The suspect was torn away from his cell halfway through his own lunch, which consisted of microwaved cottage pie and peas that were a strange grey colour. But despite the unappealing appearance of the food, Andrew had been hungry and would have finished the meal given the opportunity.

'Interview commencing at 1.53pm.' Palmer turned on the recording equipment and ran through the list of charges he had collected since their last meeting.

'Mr Wade.' Barrett had been flicking through a file and closed it, slamming it down on the table between them making Andrew startle. 'You've been busy since we last met.' Palmer did his best to disguise a smirk. 'Fancy telling us why you broke your bail conditions and left the country?'

The solicitor looked at his client and nodded.

'I was scared.' Andrew sat back in his chair, slouching and attempting to look at ease.

'Scared of what?'

'I knew you pigs'd try and pin it on me.'

The solicitor gave a little cough, wishing his client had better manners.

'And why would we do that?' Palmer asked, ignoring the pig remark. He'd heard it plenty of times during his career and he could think of worse insults.

'Because you don't have a clue who did it and I've got form. It didn't take a genius to work out you were looking at me. And…' He shifted in his seat a little. 'I wasn't exactly honest about the last time I spoke to him.'

'Why not?' Palmer's eyes narrowed.

'Because I asked him for money and he wouldn't give it to me.'

'That must have upset you,' Barrett cut in, cradling a polystyrene cup of watery coffee.

'Not really,' Andrew lied.

'Your father was happy to let you sit in prison rather than hand over a few hundred pounds and you're telling us that didn't bother you?' Palmer shook his head unconvinced.

'Well…' Andrew scratched the back of his head and then chewed his fingernails. 'I wasn't thrilled, but it's his money.'

'A witness has confirmed they were present when your father received the call from Peterborough police station on November the sixth. This witness has told us that your father was extremely upset and described his mood as "irate".'

'He was irate?' Andrew spat, a slither of his finger nail hurtling through the air. 'How do you think I felt?! I'm his only child and he wouldn't cough up a few hundred quid to help me. He was happy to leave me rot in prison. What sort of man turns his back on his son?'

'But this wasn't the first time you'd turned to your father for money, was it, Andrew? We've been through his bank statements and your prison record and Mr Wade posted bail on your behalf on a number of occasions.'

'So?' Andrew really didn't appear to understand that this was anything unusual.

'So, according to your mother, you had promised to get clean on a number of occasions.'

'It's not that easy. They never tried to understand. He was my dad. He should have helped me.' Andrew had gone from being aggressive to being defensive. His excuses were not convincing or original. Palmer and Barrett had dealt with plenty of addicts over the years and Andrew Wade was no different to the others.

'My client has written this statement.' The solicitor pushed the paper across to Palmer but Barrett snatched it up and ran his eye over it.

'Why didn't you tell us this before?' Barrett lowered the document and spoke through gritted teeth.

'I'd forgot. I was upset. My dad was dead.' He spoke with almost no conviction. 'Check. If you check with the landlord, you'll see I'm telling the truth.'

Palmer put out his hand for the statement and Barrett passed it over for him to read. It seemed that Andrew Wade had gone over to The Black Bull for a lock-in on the evening his father was murdered. Wade claimed he'd been under the influence of crystal meth and alcohol that evening and the memory had been a blur. Not wanting to admit this to the police at the time he was first interviewed by them, he pretended he'd been home alone instead. It would have been a breach of his bail conditions anyway, so he'd been keen to keep it hidden.

'When did this memory return?' Palmer put the signed document down and looked across the table flatly at Andrew.

'After the accident.' He rubbed his head. 'But by then I'd already done a runner, hadn't I.'

'We'll be checking out your statement. Until then you will have to remain in custody at Her Majesty's pleasure.' Barrett's lips tightened. 'You'll be facing charges for breach of your bail conditions, possession of a class A drug and dangerous driving, as well as the original charges of carrying a weapon and possession of a class A substance.' He stood and arranged the papers into a neat pile. 'You've really cocked up this time.' Barrett left the room.

Andrew looked more sullen than he had at the start of the interview. 'I can't help it. I'm an addict.' He turned to Palmer hoping for a glimpse of understanding.

'Then I suggest you use this next stint in prison to get clean,' Palmer said standing and started to follow his boss out of the room. 'Do it for your mother.' Palmer stopped and turned to face the man. 'She deserves better than this. It's time to grow up, Andrew.'

In the corridor Palmer found Barrett waiting for him.

'Get onto this immediately.' Barrett shoved the statement into Palmer's chest. 'Let's confirm this and move on. We've wasted enough time on Wade.'

'Seems that bump on the head might have done him some good,' he joked.

'I doubt that very much. Lost cause, that one,' Barrett said as Andrew and his solicitor appeared just in time to hear the statement echo down the corridor towards them.

'Pigs!' Andrew put his middle finger up at the inspectors before being manhandled back to his cell by two officers.

'Charming.' Palmer straightened his tie.

'We need DNA samples from Shane Matlock and Andrew Wade. Get it arranged,' Barrett instructed. 'I want to know who Wendy Matlock had sex with before her murder. There appears to be no sign of a boyfriend. It's likely she knew her attacker.'

'You think the same person she had sex with murdered her?' Palmer was surprised his boss had come to this conclusion based on very little.

'It's possible. We know our assailant is male.'

'But this killer is meticulous. I can't see him deliberately leaving DNA at the scene. It doesn't fit the profile.' Palmer shook his head.

'I've told you before, Joe, stop watching so much American TV,' Barrett teased, his eyes shining like the snow outside on the ground.

Chapter 17

Shane Matlock appeared at the station right on time. By his side stood Gemma, fiercely holding his hand. Her fake eyelashes looked heavy on her eyelids and her dyed dark hair glimmered beneath the artificial light like melted chocolate. On her shoulder was a large designer handbag, which the female officer behind reception had noticed and was sure was a fake.

'Mr Matlock.' Palmer appeared and approached the couple who sat stiffly in the waiting area. 'Thanks for coming in.'

Both Gemma and Shane stood at the same time. Palmer noticed how Gemma rested her hand on her bump for effect. As if her pregnancy might prevent them from asking Shane any difficult questions. 'We've got nothing to hide.' Gemma smiled sweetly.

'I'm afraid you will have to wait out here, Miss Nash.'

The revelation that she would not be invited in to participate in the interview was not well received. Her shiny lips pursed. and she tore her hand away from Shane's.

'What was the point in me coming?' she huffed taking a seat again and folding her arms across her ample bosom.

'This way please.' Palmer led Shane away, paying no attention to the spoilt woman who was still seething in reception.

'She's just hormonal,' Shane said wanting to excuse her brattish behaviour, guessing that Palmer wasn't approving.

'Thank you for agreeing to come and give us a DNA swab.' Palmer opened the door to a room where an official stood waiting to take the swab. 'It's so that we can eliminate you from our enquiries.'

'But I suspect my DNA is all over that house. I did used to live there.' Shane looked nervous.

'It appears the victim had sexual intercourse not long before her death,' Palmer told him flatly, watching closely for any sign of a reaction.

'Sex?' Shane blinked with surprise. 'With who?'

'That's what we intend to find out.'

Shane nodded and opened his mouth under the instruction, allowing the gloved hand to run a swab around the inside of his left cheek for a moment. The cotton wool had felt odd when it had scrapped against his teeth and he ran his tongue around his mouth, wanting to wet it again.

'That will now be sent off to the lab,' the officer said, popping the swab into a sealed container before leaving the room.

'Did Wendy have a boyfriend?' Palmer asked loosely.

'No. She did not.' Shane appeared offended by the question, which seemed odd given that his pregnant girlfriend was sitting not far away. 'She would have told me.'

'I see.' Palmer glanced down at his watch wishing the end of the day would come around quickly. 'So was she in the habit of sleeping with strangers?' He was tired and looking for a reaction.

'No,' Shane said quietly through gritted teeth. 'She was not like that.'

'But you're sure there wasn't a boyfriend?' Palmer was nonchalant.

'Certain.' Shane remained convinced.

'Strange then, that she had had sexual intercourse before her death, wouldn't you say?'

Shane blushed. 'It wasn't me.'

'That's what the test will confirm.' He let the statement hand in the air long enough for Shane to think that he might be in some doubt about it.

'Do you need me for anything else or can I go home now?' He shifted on the spot, keen to get back to his girlfriend and out of the police station.

'You're free to go.' Palmer, leaning against the desk, signalled to the door with a wave of his hand. 'Thanks for your time.' He waited for Shane to open the door and then followed him casually, making sure he didn't get lost on his way out.

When he returned to the incident room upstairs, Barrett, who had been busily talking on the phone, welcomed him.

'Shane Matlock has been in and given a DNA sample. I wouldn't be that surprised if it turns out he was still sleeping with his estranged wife; but I don't fancy him for the killings.' Palmer picked up a packet of biscuits that was lying on his desk and took one before offering them to Barrett, who politely declined.

'I've had Mrs Wade on the phone. She's keen to see Andrew. I've advised her against it. Visiting a prison is the last thing she needs. Poor woman needs closure, not further heartache.'

Barrett watched as a crumb tumbled down Palmer's chin before landing on his tie. Barrett fought a strong urge to brush it off. He hated people having a scruffy appearance. He was always well turned-out. His shirt was always ironed, his shoes shined and his silver hair kept neat. Despite the fact he was a widower he had never let it jeopardise his appearance, even if he was reminded of his beloved wife every time he got the iron and board out of the kitchen cupboard. Her death had left a gaping hole in his heart and Barrett knew he would remain a single man forever more. Besides, since he'd lived alone for the last five years, he had become accustomed to doing things his way and he was sure no woman would ever put up with his deeply embedded strange personal habits.

Since the death of his wife, Josephine, the home they had shared together remained untouched. Her clothes still hung in the wardrobe, her perfume sat on her dressing table, and the house was still her home as much as it was his. Barrett had no desire to remove her memory from his life. Having her possessions around still kept him feeling close to her, as if she might return after an unusually long holiday.

On the few occasions Palmer had seen an opportunity to go into Barrett's house, his colleague had always made excuses: the place was a mess; he was in the middle of decorating. There was always a reason why Palmer could not go inside and, as a result, Palmer found himself wondering if his boss did, in fact, live in squalor. It didn't seem likely, given the fastidious nature of the man, but it was the only explanation he could come up with. Either that or Barrett was suffering so badly from OCD that he was paranoid about introducing other people's germs into his house.

'Have you given any more thought to our offer on Christmas day?' Palmer asked with a mouthful of biscuit.

'Let's see how the case unfolds.' Barrett dreaded having to ask his team to come in on the twenty-fifth, especially those like Palmer who had children. 'Things are not exactly progressing in the way I hoped they would,' he admitted, still looking at the crumb, which sat comfortably on Palmer's tie, wishing it would tumble, or get brushed off.

'Any news on the glasses?' Palmer asked wiping more crumbs away from the corner of his mouth, understanding why Barrett hadn't given a clear answer to the invitation.

'No prints, no unusual DNA.'

'This perpetrator is good. He's organised and diligent,' he had to admit. 'I keep thinking about the note on the box left at the scene, *Now You See Me*. Is that for us or is it a message to the victim? If it is a message for the victim, why not leave it at the scene after the murder? Why take the glasses and then return them? Is it to taunt us or someone else?'

Barrett didn't like it when Palmer fired questions at him like that. He preferred order.

'At the moment we can't answer any of those questions, but what it does suggest is that killer is getting arrogant.'

'That's what I'm worried about.' Palmer clapped his hands together brushing away any excess biscuit.

'I do think that this is personal though, Joe. Somehow our killer has inserted himself into the lives of the victims. We just need to work out how and why.'

'I'm going to go back through everything we have on Dennis Wade and Wendy Matlock and see if we've missed anything.'

'Good.' Barrett nodded. 'Get Hale to help you. In the meantime, I have to interview the manager of the Army Surplus Store where Wendy worked… Jason Bagley,' he said checking his notes. 'Then there is something else I want to look into.' The cogs of his mind were turning and an idea had struck him, which had not occurred to him before.

'What is it, sir?' Palmer recognised the look on his colleague's face and was curious about what he was thinking.

'If I get anywhere with it, I'll let you know.' He tapped his nose before turning and walking into his office.

Palmer hoped he was onto something. All he wanted to do was solve the case and be home in time to spend Christmas day with his son. Looking at the clock on the incident room wall he knew he would have to cancel attending the carol service with them that night. Letting out a deep sigh Palmer picked up the phone and dialled his wife's number. He'd been looking forward to hearing his son sing for weeks and, to make matters worse, he knew his bitter disappointment would be matched by his child's. But it was his job. He didn't have a choice.

The conversation was brief and, when it ended, Palmer called Elly Hale over to help him comb through the evidence. 'Wade and Matlock,' he said turning to his screen, 'I want us to go through it all again.'

'Another late night then?' She sounded almost pleased.

'Yes. Another night away from my wife and son.' Palmer was in no mood for gentle flirting. 'Let's get this done and hopefully we might make it home before midnight.' He handed the files over without looking at her.

'Very well, sir.' Elly adopted a more serious tone and returned to her desk feeling dejected. Suddenly the prospect of being over at the CCTV control room scanning through hours of footage seemed more appealing than it had.

By half past nine she was struggling to keep her eyes open, so was both grateful and surprised when Palmer appeared holding two cups of coffee.

'Peace offering.' He handed one over, which Elly happily accepted.

'It's no bother.' She took a sip of the hot black coffee, which burnt her tongue and the inside of her lower lip. 'You're stressed. We all are,' she added, putting the coffee down.

'Still, I shouldn't bite your head off. We're all in the same boat.' Palmer put his cup down next to hers and pulled a chair up to her desk. 'Found anything?'

'Wendy Matlock had lots of hobbies.' She displayed a number of photographs to prove her point. 'She loved outdoor pursuits and was extremely active.'

Palmer waited patiently for her to get to the point.

'Dennis Wade was also somewhat obsessive. His son has told us that he spent all his time in the bookshop and very little time at home.'

'Yes,' Palmer encouraged, having no idea where she was going with it.

'Well, they are both obsessive.'

Palmer scratched his head.

'I think maybe there is something in that. Maybe the killer is punishing people who spend more time at work, or concentrating on hobbies, than they do at home. Maybe that is the link.' She sat back in her chair not knowing whether she felt triumphant or foolish.

'Okay. So you are suggesting this is about neglect?' He was trying to unpick her theory.

'Yes, or something like that.' She went to pick up her cup but changed her mind again the moment her bottom lip started to throb again. 'It fits with the words left on the glasses box too. *Now You See Me* is perhaps a message from some who feels they haven't been noticed. Someone who wants to be seen. Probably a child who was neglected by their parents.'

'Like Andrew Wade?' Palmer didn't believe he was the one responsible for the killings even if he did believe himself to be a neglected offspring.

'Someone *like* him,' Elly suggested, then sucked on her lip in an attempt to soothe it.

'It's not a bad theory.' Palmer sat back in his chair and ran his hands through his hair. 'But until we have a suspect it is only that – a theory. Piece of advice.' He lent in. 'I wouldn't run it past the DCI just yet. He's not that fond of theories.'

'In all honesty, sir, it is the only thing I've come up with. I've been through the files and I can't see anything else that links the victims.' She was exasperated. 'I can't find something that isn't there.'

'Perhaps we should speak to Andrew Wade again,' Palmer said giving some serious thought to her theory. 'I'll run it by Barrett. Good work.' He stood and patted her shoulder, letting his hand lingering there just a second or two longer than it should have done.

Chapter 18

8.30am Friday 20th December

Veronica had not slept properly since the news of Dennis's murder. It wasn't surprising that she lay in bed at night crying, with awful images of her butchered husband roaming around her head. She wanted it all to go away. She wanted it all to have been a nightmare. She wanted her husband back.

Sitting at the kitchen table in the gloom, nursing a now cold cup of tea, she stared out of the window at a plucky robin who was sifting through the snow looking for its breakfast. Veronica found herself wondering how the birds never seemed to get cold feet. Perhaps they didn't feel things in the way people did. She wished for a moment she could be like the robin.

The holly bush that grew towards the back of the garden was all but bare of its berries. The birds had taken most of them. Veronica remembered happier times when she would pick the leaves and make a wreath for the front door. There was no wreath on the Wade's front door this year. She'd been planning to make it after returning from Somerset but no longer had any desire to. With her husband dead and her son in prison, Veronica faced a bleak future alone.

She was dreading returning to her sister's house for the festive period. The plan had been to spend it at home with Dennis. Andrew, as always, had been invited but it was never certain he'd show up. Some years he did. Others he didn't. Dennis had told her to stop laying a place for him, but she never paid attention. He was her son and he would always be welcome at her table.

Veronica knew there was no way Francesca would leave her alone over Christmas and she had no choice but to go with her. Realising that she and Francesca were due to go to Heathrow Airport in two days' time, Veronica was determined to try and see her son before she left. She wanted answers. She wanted to hug him and hit him. She needed to look into his eyes and understand how they had ended up here.

When she heard the floorboards creaking above her head, and the sound of Francesca beginning to rise, Veronica went over to the phone in the hallway and dialled the Parkside Police Station number. DCI Barrett had told her yesterday that he would put her in touch with the prison but he had not called her back. She hit the numbers on the handset with irritation, feeling both powerless and frustrated.

As she waited for the call to be answered Veronica noticed her reflection in the mirror. Her hair was unkempt and needed washing. The nightdress she wore hung off her figure, looking looser than before. Beneath her hazel eyes were sunken bags and the skin on her face looked grey. She didn't recognise the woman staring back at her. Who was this stranger? Where had Veronica gone? With a shaking hand she slowly tried to smooth her wild hair. Dennis always liked her looking her best. What would he think if he saw her now?

Just as the station answered the call Veronica decided to hang up. She did want to see Andrew, but she was determined to show up looking like his mother and not some bag lady. She pushed past Francesca who was padding down the stairs and locked herself in the bathroom.

'Is everything okay?' Francesca called up the stairs.

There was no response.

'Veronica?'

'What! I just want to have a bath in peace, if that's alright with you.' The venom in her sister's voice took her by surprise. 'Oh, and I am not going to Somerset until I've seen and spoken to Andrew. Is that clear?' The bellowing from the other side of the door made Francesca feel wobbly on the stairs.

'Yes.' She stared up at the closed door. 'Whatever you like. I was just about to make some breakfast. Can I get you anything?'

'Do we have any sausages?'

'I don't know.' Francesca was both shocked and relieved that her sister actually wanted to eat something. She'd more or less given up on food over the last week.

'Sausage sandwich, if we have some. If not, I'll pop out later.' The determination in Veronica's voice had returned and Francesca found herself wanting to cry with joy.

'You have your bath. I'll pop out if we need anything,' Francesca called from the bottom of the stairs as she wiped a single tear from her cheek.

***

At Parkside, the incident room was a flurry of activity. It turned out that the annual Army Surplus Store Christmas party had taken place on the night of Saturday the fourteenth of December. The store employees had been taken to Pizza Express for supper followed by drinks at The Regal, a downtrodden Wetherspoon pub close to Parker's Piece. After interviewing the general manager, Jason Bagley, an ex-army officer who had done tours of both Iraq and Afghanistan, Barrett had learnt about the Christmas party. It seems they ate at seven and were at the pub from about eight o'clock onwards. As far as Jason could remember – although he struggled, given the number of pints and whisky chasers he'd had – he believed that Wendy left the pub around half past ten or eleven. Jason wasn't certain she left alone and had some vague recollection of her chatting to a man at the bar at some point during the evening.

Barrett had quickly called Singh, who was already at the CCTV control room, and asked him to check the cameras in the area from that night. It hadn't taken Singh very long to find footage of Wendy leaving The Regal, tottering along the icy pavement and making her way to the nearest taxi rank. Footage from another camera showed her talking to a man wearing a hooded coat for some time, before the pair got into a taxi together.

Having seen the footage of Wendy and the man, Barrett and Palmer were convinced it was the same person who had been caught on CCTV leaving the area of the bookshop in the early hours after Dennis Wade's murder. Although the police were already convinced that the killer responsible for both murders was the same person, they now had concrete proof. The only problem being that the man's face was hidden from view in both instances.

Palmer had been tasked with calling the taxi company and trying to identify which driver had picked the victim and the suspect up and what their destination had been. After a few calls backwards and forwards between the friendly woman at the taxi depot, a number of drivers and the police, they finally established that a driver called Mohammed Okeke took the job. Mohammed, who had a limited grasp of the English language, finally agreed to come into the station to give a statement. As soon as the interview time was set, Palmer busied himself arranging for a police sketch artist to be there. It was a long shot, given that it was nearly a week since the driver had picked the pair up and had likely encountered plenty of other strangers in between, but it was a new lead and the team felt spurred on.

Once they had established that Okeke was originally from Nigeria, and had only been in Britain for the last twelve months, it was decided, to save time, that they would bring a translator in to help with the interview. Barrett knew that the finer details relating to the description of the suspect might otherwise get lost with the language barrier. But, as was the case with a lot of police procedures, it was not that easy finding a translator and a sketch artist who could both come to Cambridge and sit in on an interview at the same time.

Barrett, who knew exactly how to play the system, quickly got on to his boss and explained the situation. It was in everyone's interest to solve the case as swiftly as possible, especially given the swarm of journalists who had descended on the snow-covered city and who were stirring up fear among local residents. Even shopkeepers had reported the quietest December on their books in years. People were scared.

The Chief Superintendent had immediately got onto his contacts at the Met in London and asked them to help. Within two hours Barrett received a call telling him that a sketch artist and translator would be arriving in Cambridge at six o'clock that evening, just in time to sit in on the interview with Mohammed Okeke. At last, Barrett and Palmer felt like they might be getting somewhere.

The task of sending the footage of Wendy and the suspect and the footage of the character leaving the area after Dennis Wade's murder to a computer forensics analyst had fallen to Elly Hale. The police needed to know whether forensics could confirm if the hooded character in both recordings was, in fact, the same person. It appeared to the inspector that it was a given. The coat worn in both pieces of film was identical but, in order to build a case, they needed confirmation from paid specialists. Barrett and Palmer's guesswork would not stand up in court.

Not only were the team swamped with the murder cases but also it seemed a gang of thieves were working in the area, breaking into some of the more desirable homes in the city and robbing them. The gang was spray painting the walls of the houses and destroying everything they could. There was always an increase of thefts at Christmas time but neither Barrett nor Palmer had ever witnessed such destructive behaviour during robberies. The families of those burgled houses were now facing a miserable Christmas. The thieves appeared to be taking special pleasure in destroying all the Christmas decorations in the houses they broke into. The local press had nicknamed the criminals The Grinch Gang and the pressure was mounting on the Cambridge Constabulary to bring those responsible to justice, as well as to apprehend a sadistic killer who still stalked the streets.

Mohammed arrived at six ten, running late after a long driving shift. Typically, his last job of the day had been a long-distance journey to Harlow. If he'd been familiar with the term sod's law he would have chuckled to himself.

He lived in a small flat on the outskirts of the town with his wife and three children. The house was small and the rent, in his opinion, was expensive. His wife worked part-time for a cleaning company that dealt with businesses rather than family homes. The pair had left Nigeria wanting a better life for their children but had not yet entirely settled into their new existence. The children had found their feet, the way children do, but the parents were struggling with the language and the awful weather. It was the first time any member of the family had ever seen snow. Until recently it was something that had only existed in books and on television.

Mohammed had spent a small fortune on suitable coats, hats and gloves for the family. He had taken them all to TK Maxx, a designer outlet store off Newmarket Road. The children had run around the store with glee, running their hands over the rails of clothes. His wife, who was a reserved woman, spent her time checking every price tag before deciding what she and the children would purchase.

Standing in Parkside Police Station, Mohammed wished he was at home. It had been a long day and he wanted to be in his kitchen tucking in to one of his wife's Nigerian stews. Her cooking always reminded him of home and made him feel happy. Working as a taxi driver wasn't his ambition and he struggled to cope with the drunks he found himself ferrying on Friday and Saturday nights. On more than one occasion he had ended up cleaning sick from the back seats of his Ford people carrier. It was not the life he had envisaged, but his children were happy and getting a good education; so, like any good father, he carried on regardless and made sure to smile.

When Barrett and Palmer arrived in reception to welcome him he gave a warm handshake. All day, he'd been doing his best to try to remember the face of the man he was there to describe. He remembered noticing the face that night, because there was something unusual about it, but he couldn't put his finger on what it was that was strange.

'Thank you for coming.' Palmer could tell the man was nervous. 'Please come this way.'

Palmer led the way to the interview room followed by Mohammed and Barrett. Inside, the sketch artist and interpreter were waiting patiently. The problem with Mohammed's English wasn't that he didn't have a good grasp of the language but rather his accent and pronunciation made it hard for some to understand. Given that his description of the suspect would play a key part in the case, the inspectors both thought the presence of the interpreter was worthwhile.

The interview didn't take long. Mohammed explained that he'd collected Wendy and the suspect from the taxi rank near St Andrew, the Great Church on Regent Street, and had driven them both to New Barn in Ickleton. He told the inspectors that he thought she appeared rather drunk. The male, whose face Mohammed only saw briefly, had sat in the taxi facing the boot of the car. Barrett felt his heart sink with that disclosure, but as Mohammed recounted the details concerning the suspect's height, and a description of the coat the man was wearing, he allowed himself a glimmer of hope.

With awe and fascination Barrett and Palmer remained silent when the sketch artist started work. After an hour they had an E-fit of their suspect, but Mohammed wasn't entirely happy.

'It was sort of like that,' he said frowning at the picture. 'Difficult to remember. So many faces I see.' He adjusted his porkpie hat.

'You've been extremely helpful.' Barrett shook Mohammed's hand enthusiastically before showing the gentleman back to reception.

'So, we have our man,' Palmer said holding the sketch and examining it.

'We have *a* man,' Barrett corrected.

'He looks like any bloke on the street. Nothing remarkable about him. It's not even that clear from the image what age he is. Could be thirty. Could be fifty.'

'We got a good description of the coat.' Barrett refused to be downbeat.

'Yes. Dark blue duffle,' Palmer recounted following Barrett up the stairs to the incident room. 'Do you want me to get this out to the press?'

'Quick as you can. And find an image of a coat similar to the one Mr Okeke described, too. I want those images in circulation in every paper and on all the local news channels. Let's tighten the net on this creep.'

'I'll get onto it tonight, sir.' Palmer looked at the clock on the wall and knew there was no chance he'd be home in time to tuck his son into bed.

***

The man walked along the edge of the water, carrying a small torch. It was dark and the temperature was minus two degrees. His breathing was heavy as he hunted for the person he had arranged to meet that night.

The moon reflected in the ripples of the water and a canopy of stars blanketed the night sky above.

Standing near a tree in the distance the man saw the person he was looking for. His heartbeat quickened as the closeness between their bodies lessened. He knew this day had been coming for a long time, but he didn't know why it had taken so long.

'Who are you?' The man said between deep breaths.

'Someone who knows what you did,' the man spat.

'Why here, why now?'

The silhouetted figure looked up at the universe and pondered a moment.

'Because I can and because I should,' he said as he produced a large crowbar from behind his back and brought it swinging into the skull of his companion.

Chapter 19

At Parkside Police Station the phones would not stop ringing. After the morning news had been aired, showing the sketch of the suspect and the image of the coat, the station had been inundated with calls. Unsurprisingly, it seemed lots of people knew a man in his early to mid- thirties who wore a similar coat and who lived in the area, but not one single caller had been able to say with absolute certainty that the sketch fitted the face of the person they were calling in to report.

Nonetheless, the officers manning the phones took down the name of each person and promised to investigate. By eleven o'clock they had a list of over eighty names.

Palmer, who was keen to start sifting through the names, was interrupted by a call from the front desk.

'Sir, I have a woman here who'd like to report a missing person.'

'I'll send Singh down to talk to her.' Palmer slammed the phone down and summoned Singh from the other side of the room. 'Missing person has been reported. I need you to go and take a statement. Crack on with it though, Singh, we need everyone working on this case.'

'Yes.' Singh jumped to attention and took himself downstairs to speak to the woman.

Sitting on a chair wringing her hands, sat a woman with red eyes and a blotchy face.

'Sergeant Singh,' he introduced himself. 'Come this way.'

The troubled woman stood and shuffled along behind, dabbing her eyes with a soggy tissue.

'How can I help?' Singh held the door open and showed the woman into the interview room.

'My Eddie, he's missing. He didn't come home last night.'

'Can I take your name?' Singh sat down and removed a pen and pad from his white shirt pocket.

'Mrs Susan Kilpatrick.' She sniffed and sat down opposite the officer.

'Where do you live?'

'We live at 79 Bridewell Road in Fulbourn. Near the psychiatric hospital.' She spoke as if saying the words might somehow affect her sanity.

'And who is it you are reporting missing?' Singh remained patient.

'My husband Eddie. Edward Kilpatrick.'

'When did you last see your husband?' His pen was poised over the notepad.

'Yesterday afternoon. Probably at about four.' She dabbed her eyes again. 'He said he was going to the shops to get something for dinner but he never came home. I've tried calling his mobile and he isn't answering. It's not like him to disappear. Our daughter is arriving from London later on today. He wouldn't miss that for the world. I'm worried he's been in an accident.'

'So he was driving?'

'Yes, he took his car. I thought it was a bit odd at the time because the supermarket is a short walk from the house. But then again with the weather being what it is…' She trailed off.

'What's the make and model?'

'It's a brown Volvo estate.'

'What does your husband do for work?' Singh was going through the motions.

'He's running for council.' Susan beamed with pride. 'It's been his ambition to get involved in politics, so when he retired from his recruitment firm last year–'

'What was he wearing?' Singh interrupted as quickly and as politely as he could.

'He had on a pair of blue corduroy trousers, a beige checked shirt and a green jumper. And his coat, one of those waxy dark green things.'

'Have you tried calling the hospitals?'

'No.' She looked at him blankly while her fingers fiddled with the tissue in her hand.

'Right. Please wait here a moment, Mrs Kilpatrick, while I make a few calls. Can I get you a hot drink while you wait?'

'Thank you. A tea would do nicely. Two sugars.'

Singh could see she had kind eyes.

'I'll send someone to bring you tea,' Singh said closing the door and letting out a sigh. This was not the case he wanted to be working on.

Singh returned to the interview room, accompanied by a FLO, just as Susan was finishing off her cup of tea.

'This is Julie. She's a family liaison officer.' Julie smiled warmly at the distressed woman. 'I've been in touch with the hospitals and no man fitting your husband's description has been admitted. I've put an APB out on the car. What we'll need from you, please, Mrs Kilpatrick, is a photograph of your husband so that we can circulate his image, which will take place within forty-eight hours from now. In the meantime, Julie will take you home. If you can please give her anything that has your husband's DNA on it, like a toothbrush or comb, that would be very helpful. Also, please create a list of regular places or address that your husband frequented so that we can start a search.'

Susan thanked the sergeant, who was keen to return to the incident room, as she was led away by Julie.

'Missing persons case filed, sir,' Singh informed Palmer as he looked at the clock and realised it still wasn't quite lunchtime. 'Probably just a cheating spouse who's done a runner.'

'Good. I want to you go through these.' Palmer handed a list of names to Singh. 'Let me know if anything interesting shows up.'

'Sir!' From across the room Elly Hale shouted, waving at Barrett who looked up from his desk, unimpressed at being summoned in such a way.

The rest of the officers turned and stared. When Barrett saw the look of excitement on the sergeant's face, and when he realised she was clinging to a phone, obviously still in the middle of a call, he leapt out of his chair and went to where Elly was standing. Her eyes were bright and her deep-red painted nails gripped the handset held tightly to her chest.

'I've got a journalist calling from the *Cambridge News* head office in Waterbeach. They've had a delivery, sir. A box arrived addressed to the paper. The editor has just opened it and called us immediately. The box had three fingers in it.'

'Three?' He knew what this meant, and he didn't like it one little bit. 'Tell him not to touch a thing.' Barrett waggled his finger. 'Get forensics over there now. Do we know how the package was delivered?'

'It was discovered on the front step outside the entrance to the office. No one saw who put it there.'

'Tell them not to touch it,' Barrett repeated. 'And tell them that no one is to come or go from the office. I want to speak to everyone on site.'

'Yes, sir. Just one more thing, there was a note.' Elly's expression was grave. 'It simply said, ...*Now You Don't.*'

***

The journey from Balsham to Highpoint South Prison, on the outskirts of Stradishall village on the Cambridgeshire–Suffolk borders, seemed to take forever. The slush on the roads meant that traffic was forced to crawl slowly. During most of the year the gridlock in Cambridge was unbearable, but with Christmas and the weather both looming every journey took even longer.

Veronica sat alone in the back of the taxi, her hands clasped together as she looked out at the bleak country fields. A heavy grey sky loomed above threatening rain any moment.

As the car finally pulled up the reality of the situation dawned on her. The tall barbed wire fence that surrounded the vast red brick building was as welcoming as the weather. Veronica swallowed and picked her handbag up from beside her feet, gripping the leather as if her life depended on it. The fact that the prison had once been home to Myra Hindley sent shivers down her spine.

She paid the fare, thanked the driver, who looked at her suspiciously, and got out of the car. As the gate slammed shut behind her and the metal lock snapped into place Veronica felt her legs turn to jelly. She never thought she'd be back in a place like this again. Andrew had vowed to her that he would turn his life around and now all those empty promises came back to taunt her.

Once she'd been through security, and made to feel like a criminal herself, she was shown to the visiting room where Andrew was already sat at a table waiting. He looked worse for wear. The cuts on his face from the accident were taking their time to heal. Her son, who she'd always thought of as a big man, now appeared small and shrunken in the grey tracksuit which the prison had issued. Across his chest he wore a bright yellow band like a mark of shame.

'Andrew.' She sat on the cold plastic chair opposite unable to reach out and hug her son. Her eyes searched his face for answers, but he remained tight lipped, refusing to look at her. 'How did we get here?'

Slowly he turned to face his mother, his eyelids flittering for a moment, before he shrugged. 'I dunno what you want me to say?' He had no fight left in him.

'Say something, anything. Just tell me what you were thinking running away like that?' Her voice shook.

'I knew the pigs would try and finger me for this.' His eyes burnt with anger. 'I was just looking after myself.'

'Why didn't you tell the truth about the argument with your father? It would have saved everyone so much heartache.' She sighed.

'I didn't want you to know about it. I didn't want you to know I'd fucked up again.'

'Language.' She frowned.

'I didn't want you thinking I'd failed.' He paused. 'Again.'

'But you must have realised I'd find out. And you think by running away you were doing me a favour?' she said almost laughing.

'I understood it didn't look good,' Andrew admitted chewing his lip. 'But I didn't do it.'

'I know that, you silly boy.' His mother hissed. 'But rather than tell the truth you decided to break the law. You've caused me more pain than you will ever know. I needed you, Andrew. I needed to be with my son.' This was the first time in their relationship that either of them had ever spoken so openly. It was a revelation to Veronica. She felt good telling her son how she felt. 'I know you and your father never really saw eye to eye. You are very different people.'

Andrew considered correcting her tense but decided against it. He was in enough trouble with her already.

'By running away you made yourself look guilty. Do you know how I struggled with that?' Andrew hung his head, not wanting to hear any more. 'I feel like I've lost you as well as your father. What have I done to deserve this? Please, tell me what I've done?'

'I didn't kill the bastard,' Andrew suddenly erupted. 'But you're acting as if this is all my fault. Like you always do. Like he always did.'

'That's not fair.' She spoke more quietly, trying to calm the conversation. 'We both love you.'

Andrew put his head in his hands. 'You know what, Ma, I think maybe you do, but I know that he never did.'

A long silence filled the space between them. Veronica reached out her hand across the table and for a while Andrew just looked at it.

'Your father loved you. He just wasn't very good at showing it.' This was the excuse Veronica had used time and time again.

'You think he loved you?' Andrew asked. Veronica went quiet. 'Because all he ever did was spend time in that bookshop or on his hobbies. He didn't love anyone except himself. I'm glad he's dead.'

Those four words cut through Veronica's heart like a knife.

'Go home, Ma,' he said finally.

'I'm all you've got.' Her eyes filled with tears. 'Don't do this. Don't give up on me.'

'It's too late. Give up. I'm going down for a proper stretch this time. Get on with your life and forget about me.'

'You are all I have left. Don't ask me to lose you and your father. I couldn't stand it. I don't care about your mistakes. You are my son. I love you.'

'Then God help you,' Andrew said looking coldly at his mother.

'If you do this, and sever ties with me…' Veronica's resolve returned, along with a steely look in her eyes, as she continued, 'Then God help you because, quite frankly, my son, no one else will.'

***

Barrett and Palmer raced to the *Cambridge News* office in Waterbeach in their unmarked car with the siren screaming. The traffic parted way in the city centre like the Red Sea had for Moses as the Volvo saloon hurtled along the gritted roads and out into countryside.

'Three fingers,' Palmer said, keeping a close eye on the road for ice. Under most circumstances it would not have been wise to travel at that speed given the conditions.

'That's what they said,' Barrett replied gravely.

'Why send it to the paper?'

'This killer wants attention, Joe. What better way to get it?'

'Killing two, or maybe three, people isn't enough? What more does this madman want?'

'That's what we need to figure out. This killer is playing a game and so far, he's always been one step ahead.' It pained Barrett to admit it as the car pulled into the business park and up outside the newspaper headquarters. The journey had taken them double the amount of time it should due to the Christmas gridlock in the city.

Both men jumped out and approached the glass entrance where an officer stood guard making sure no one entered or left. Without speaking both inspectors flashed their badges and the bulky man moved aside.

Once inside the modern building the inspectors were led to the second floor where the *Cambridge News* had its headquarters. The room was sparsely furnished with a few desks. More officers were inside already talking statements from a couple of the journalists.

'Which one is the editor?' Barrett interrupted an interview taking place.

'There, sir.' The officer pointed to a desk in a glass box office on the far side of the room.

With purpose, Barrett marched, followed closely by Palmer, across the room. All eyes fell on them.

Without knocking Barrett pushed the door open and stepped inside. Behind a desk was a balding man in his late forties, who sat in his chair holding his head.

'We'll take it from here,' Palmer told the officer who was standing beside the editor's desk.

'DCI Barrett, and this is DI Palmer.' Barrett coughed, attempting to get the man to look up from the floor. 'We need to ask you some questions.' On the far side of the desk sat the box they were there for. Knowing what was inside made Palmer's stomach turn.

'I don't know anything, but I'll tell you what I can.' The editor looked up, his face a pale shade of green. Palmer noticed a bin splashed with vomit at the editor's feet.

'You are Mr Jeremy Roth, is that right?' Palmer asked, having made a mental note of the nameplate on the office door.

'Yes, I'm he.' The man wiped his mouth, conscious there may still be sick on his lips and chin, while Barrett pulled on a pair of nitrile gloves and moved towards the box.

It was the same size as the cardboard box that had contained the spectacles. The difference this time was not only that the box had been addressed to 'The Editor of the Cambridge News' but that the note, ...*Now You Don't*, had been written on a strip of paper placed inside the box along with the three fingers.

'When did you receive the package?' Palmer asked, grateful that Barrett had taken the decision to deal with the box.

'It was sitting outside the entrance to the building when I arrived this morning.' Jeremy swallowed another wave of nausea. 'I had a lot of work to do and forgot about it until about quarter to eleven, which was when I opened it. I thought it might be a gift.' His face was full of shame.

'Do you recognise the handwriting?' Barrett said. He used a pencil to lift the lid of the box.

'No.' Jeremy turned away not wanting to watch and covered his mouth with his shaking hand. 'Please, can you please just take it out of here.'

'Did you touch anything inside the box?' Barrett asked, ignoring the distressed man's plea.

'I took the note out and read it. The fingers...' He shuddered. 'Were beneath a piece of bubble wrap. That's over there. I didn't touch them.' He pointed to the discarded wrapping on the floor.

'Do you have any idea why this would be sent to you?' Palmer asked looking at the vomit stains on Jeremy's beige cable-knit jumper.

'No idea at all.' The editor looked lost. 'What does it mean?'

Palmer and Barrett looked at one another. The details about the fingers being removed from Wendy Matlock and Dennis Wade had been kept from the press and it was now obvious the killer wanted it out in the open.

'We believe this may be linked to a case we are currently investigating.' Barrett closed the lid of the box and retrieved the discarded bubble wrap from the floor.

'You mean those two murders?' Jeremy's dark brown eyes widened from behind his reading glasses. Palmer thought he looked more like a science teacher than a journalist.

'I'm not at liberty to comment,' Barrett said, knowing full well that by that afternoon the editor would have released the news about the fingers via the newspaper's website and that tomorrow morning there would be a front page spread and soon it would be national news.

But that was exactly what Barrett wanted to happen. He was keen to give this killer what he wanted in the hope of luring him out. He knew the Chief Superintendent wouldn't approve but Barrett had already decided he would play dumb.

Removing a few forensic bags from his inside coat pocket Barrett proceeded to bag the box in one and the bubble wrap in another. The note, which lay abandoned on the desk, was placed inside a third. He handed the bags to an officer who stood to attention near the door.

'Get this over to forensics.' The officer nodded and disappeared carrying the gruesome evidence.

'We'll need you to come to the station and make a statement,' Barrett told Jeremy while removing his gloves.

'Do you think I'm in danger?' It suddenly occurred to the editor that he had been singled out by a cold bloodied killer.

'I doubt it,' Barrett said with little sympathy, 'but we will assign an officer to you for now.'

'I'd really like to call my wife,' Jeremy asked Palmer, realising that Barrett was a cold fish. 'Just to warn her I might be home late.'

'I see no problem with that.' Palmer gave permission. 'But I would ask that you don't mention any details about the contents of the box you received at this time.'

'Fine by me. If I never think about that again, it would be too soon,' Jeremy said reaching for the mobile that lay on his desk and speed-dialling his home; even though, in his head, he was already writing the headline for the online article he would be publishing later on that day. *Killer points finger at me. Yes,* Jeremy smiled to himself for the first time since discovering the body parts, *that would do nicely.*

Chapter 20

6.00pm Saturday 21st December

Jane sat stiffly in the pub alone, sipping an orange juice and checking the time. The others were late, which she couldn't abide. It had been over a week since Dennis's murder and the future of their jobs were still on the line. Understandably Mrs Wade, who was now the owner of the shop, hadn't given much thought to what she wanted to do with the premises. Jane understood that she should be given time and space to grieve, but in the meantime a number of people were left in limbo not knowing whether they still had employment or not.

It had been Jane's idea to call a meeting with her colleagues to discuss their predicament. She had also invited Marcus, the company accountant, along, hoping that he might be able to apply some gentle pressure on the Wade family. She suspected he was Dennis's executor and that, therefore, he had the power to help.

Jane had not been able to reach Tilly, not for lack of trying, but had spoken to Marcus, Steven, Amber, Myleene and Aiden, all of whom had agreed a meeting to discuss their predicament was a good idea. The only thing Jane hadn't been able to control was where they met. She'd suggested a coffee house but after receiving a number of emails suggesting a pub instead, she had given in and agreed to go to The Maypole pub close to Jesus Green. Jane had quietly noted that three of the employees were happy to meet to grumble about their jobs being on the line but had not bothered to get involved with the wreath she had organised earlier in the week. Some people could be so selfish.

The Maypole, which stood in a quiet corner of the city, was a local institution. It was frequented by students and locals alike and remained undiscovered by most of the tourists who visited the city. It was well loved but mostly as a result of the great Italian food it served and the vast choice of gins and ales. Jane wasn't a big drinker and would have felt more at home in the coffee shop she had originally proposed.

She sat with her back facing the rest of the room and the other punters and watched out the window, waiting for her colleagues to arrive. The first to appear was Marcus, sauntering along the pavement trying to avoid the slush with his pointed leather shoes. Around his neck was a tightly woven, extremely expensive, cashmere scarf.

'Sorry I'm late,' Marcus said, kissing the air on either side of Jane's cheeks, which was something she loathed, 'traffic is awful. May I get you another drink?' He looked at her half full glass of juice.

'No thank you,' she replied curtly and sat down to watch for the others.

Marcus headed for the bar where a young man who had a large handlebar moustache welcomed him.

'A glass of Chablis.' Marcus' eyes widened, enjoying the handsome man in his vision.

By six twenty everyone had arrived and the six of them crowed round the small pub table.

Myleene and Amber nattered quietly among themselves, both occasionally glancing up at the attractive barman and giggling. Steven and Aiden chatted about the latest football scores while sipping their pints, leaving Jane and Marcus sitting in an uncomfortable silence.

Detesting the relaxed atmosphere around the table, Jane cleared her throat loudly until everyone fell silent. 'Thank you for coming. I think we should discuss the reason we are all here.' Her wild hair shone orange beneath the dimmed artificial light. 'Would anyone like to start?'

Marcus twiddled with the edge of his scarf, looking around the table at the others who all remained quiet.

'Very well.' Jane was secretly pleased she had a platform. 'I'll begin.' Worried about Aiden's pint glass falling, despite the fact it was a good few inches from the edge, she pushed it into the centre of the table. 'We have all been upset by the recent events at the bookshop.'

'And everything that has happened since,' Marcus gently reminded her, not wanting the brutal murder of Wendy Matlock to be brushed under the carpet.

'Yes, and the rest.'

'Yes,' Myleene chirped up with her broad Cambridgeshire accent. 'Did you all see that stuff on the Internet?'

The group shook their heads.

'Well, today…' She leant in, fiddling with the blond plait which fell across her shoulder. 'I was on Facebook, you know just messaging friends and the like, and it came up on my news feed.' Myleene's big blue eyes looked like glass marbles, reflecting the street light from the lamp outside the window. 'Some local paper guy got sent some human fingers in the post.' She sat back triumphantly, looking almost titillated by the revelation.

'My dear,' Marcus said with a fake smile, 'what has that got to do with this?'

'Oh yeah, well the fingers were taken from the people being killed round here.'

It took Marcus a moment or two for the words to sink in.

'You mean Dennis?' The horror was tattooed on his face.

'Yeah, that's what I'm saying. The paper said there were three fingers in a box or something. Grim huh?'

The table remained silent for a few moments.

'Some sicko is really having a field day.' Aiden frowned.

'That's bad,' Amber piped up. Until then, she'd only spoken to Myleene.

'Yeah, that's what I thought,' Myleene said taking a gulp of her coke.

'Three fingers?' Aiden asked. 'I thought only two people had died?'

'No one died,' Marcus suddenly hissed, 'they were murdered.'

'Blimey.' Steven picked up his pint and drained the dregs. 'Poor old Dennis.'

'I'd say,' said Aiden nodding in agreement.

'This isn't right, talking about these people like this. We should leave the police to their job and concentrate on ours for a moment.' Jane's lack of humanity stunned the table.

'Right, so back to business then?' Steven said with a smirk.

'I don't like your tone.' Jane turned to him with a cold stare.

'And I don't much like yours.' Marcus stroked the stem on his wine glass and looked at Jane.

'Gossiping about the gruesome details of the murders won't get us anywhere. I can't stand to think about it. We'd be better off talking about the future of our employment, which was the entire reason I arranged this meeting.' Jane still appeared unmoved by the discovery.

'Fine,' Aiden sighed, 'let's get on with it. Say what you want to say Jane.'

'I would like to ask Marcus if he knows what will happen to the shop.' The snide expression on her face was there for them all to see.

'Veronica Wade is the sole beneficiary. I think it is far too soon for me to put pressure on her to make a decision about the future of the shop.' Marcus was enjoying dangling this over Jane, although he had no desire to irritate the rest of them.

'Are you still involved in that charity? What was it, the one for young homeless men?' Jane held her head high on her long neck and allowed a small smile to settle in the corners of her mouth.

'What does that have to do with anything?' Marcus snipped back.

'Wasn't Dennis involved too?' She cocked her head.

'Briefly.' Marcus straightened in his seat and readjusted his scarf.

'I was sure he said something about leaving a substantial sum in his will. He was very proud of the work he'd done,' she sneered.

'He was. Dennis had a good heart.' The implication was clear that Jane did not.

'Do you know how long the shop is going to be shut for?' Myleene asked.

'That is police business. There is no reason they would inform me. I suspect they will be in touch with Veronica Wade in due course.' Marcus stood, announcing he was ready to leave. 'If that's all…'

'So you're unable to tell us if we still have employment?' Jane also stood blocking the exit.

'As I have already confirmed, this is a matter for the police and Mrs Wade.' Marcus took a step left and slid behind Aiden's chair, making his escape.

'I have a mortgage to pay. I can't wait to see if my job is still available in a month's time. Besides, are we even getting paid this month? We deserve answers.'

'I'm sure Mrs Wade will deal with this in due course,' Marcus sighed.

'Well you may not need a regular income but I do,' Myleene said what the rest of them had been thinking.

'If it will help, I will speak to Veronica. I'm sure you will be paid at the end of the month as usual.' He was beginning to think that agreeing to come to the pub had been a very bad idea.

'And after that?' Jane's voice screeched as Marcus ignored her question before slipping out into the cold.

'Let him go,' Steven said getting up to go over to the bar for another pint. 'It's not really his fault.'

'Don't you care about your job?' Jane asked trying to mask her disgust.

'Not really, Jane.' He turned and shrugged. 'What will be will be.'

'Well I care deeply about mine.' She removed her woollen cape from the back of her chair and flung it around her tall slender body. The fabric was a similar shade to her hair. 'I think you should be ashamed of yourselves,' Jane told the rest of the table before flouncing out.

'You know Mrs Wade's son was arrested? He's in prison,' Aiden added, stroking his ginger beard as Steven returned carrying a tray of drinks for them all.

'Yeah, I saw that on the news,' Myleene confirmed with a grimace.

'Mrs Wade must be very sad,' Amber said quietly, picking a piece of fluff from her cream jumper off her skinny black jeans.

'Poor sod.' Steven shook his head while bringing a pint of rich coloured bitter to his lips. 'Some people seem to be born with bad luck.'

Chapter 21

Palmer was tired. He'd had a bad night. His son, who was extremely over-excited about Christmas, had woken up every few hours and come in to his parents' room to see if Father Christmas had been yet. Yawning, Palmer stood by the coffee machine waiting for a hot cup of fuel. In the glass window he caught a glimpse of his reflection. He'd stopped taking care of himself. The case had taken over and his appearance was suffering. His stubble was scruffy and his shirt not as pristine as he would normally like. It seemed that there were more lines around his eyes than there had been before Dennis Wade's murder.

Elly arrived next to him, waiting her turn to get a coffee and he snapped out of his thoughts.

'Morning.' She smiled.

'Morning.' Palmer stifled another yawn.

'Something is going on.' She pointed over to Barrett who was completely wrapped up in a conversation on the phone, his brow furrowed as he jotted down notes.

'This killer certainly likes to keep us on our feet.' Palmer sipped the watery coffee. 'Why change MO at this stage? Why send the finger of the third body before we've found it? It doesn't make sense.'

'Psychopath,' Elly suggested.

'Well yes, but what is the end game? What do they want?'

'You mean apart from to kill?' Her eyes blinked and a smile fell on her lips.

'Yes. Mark my words there is a link between these victims. Something. Perhaps your neglect idea will come to fruition.' He smiled back at her and their eyes met. 'Anyway.' Palmer looked away. 'Hopefully the third victim will be on file so we can track them down quickly.'

'Do you think the third victim is alive?'

'It's certainly possible. We have to work on that assumption for now. Our job is to find them either way, but working on the idea that victim three is alive means we really need to find them as soon as possible. Time isn't on our side, given how quickly this killer disposed of the first two victims.'

'Yes, they are certainly working fast,' Elly agreed as she made her way back to her desk.

Barrett, who had hung up the phone, bellowed across the room to Singh making the rest of the office stop and turn.

'We have a DNA match on the finger,' Barrett stood and announced. 'Mr Edward Kilpatrick.'

Singh raised his eyebrows and let out a long puff of air from his lips. 'He was reported missing by his wife on Saturday morning,' Singh shared with the room. 'He left home on Friday afternoon and never returned.'

'Right. I want everyone on this. We need to find Mr Kilpatrick. That is our top priority now.'

'Joe.' Barrett pointed at Palmer with his pen. 'I want you to go speak to the wife. Find out if there is any link between Kilpatrick and the other victims. I want a search of his premises. Hale, Singh, I want you here trawling through his phone records and bank statements. Get onto the phone company and see if we can get a ping from his phone. I want his last known position. Okay, that's it. Get to work.'

Barrett approached Palmer. 'I'll come with you to speak to the wife,' he said tucking his pen into his inside jacket pocket. 'Until we have evidence of the contrary, Eddie Kilpatrick is alive, is that clear?'

'Yes, sir.' Palmer nodded. 'I presume we have to tell her about the finger?'

'We do,' Barrett said gravely. 'I'm afraid we do.'

***

Veronica stood looking out of the front window of her living room at the street she'd lived on for the last twenty years. It hadn't changed much in all that time. Some people had come and gone but otherwise it was unchanged.

She thought about her local friends, the school Andrew had attended down the road and the playground where her husband had taught their son to ride his bike. The place was awash with memories, some good and some bad. The one constant thing in her life had been Dennis but now he was gone.

Behind her Francesca was getting her bags ready. Before too long they were due to leave meet Natalie at Heathrow.

'Is everything alright?' Francesca called from the hallway.

Veronica didn't know the answer to that question. If she said yes, then she'd be lying; but if she answered no, then she'd have to acknowledge exactly what it was she was contemplating.

'I'm just thinking,' she said finally and that was the truth. She was wondering if she could go on living in the house she'd shared with Dennis, the place that held so many memories of her son.

When she'd walked away from the prison, she'd let a little piece of herself die when accepting that her relationship with her son was over. Veronica knew in her bones that she would never see him again. A switch had been thrown and there was no turning back. What kind of mother was she? What kind of son was he?

Standing in the living room, Veronica acknowledged that from that moment on she would be alone. No sister, niece or friend could ever fill the space left by her son and husband. She would always have a huge empty space in her heart, and what she realised was that being in Balsham would only act as a constant reminder.

'I'm going to sell the house,' Veronica said turning to pick up the cat, which was rubbing his body against her ankles. 'And the shop,' she added as an after-thought. 'There is nothing left for me here except memories. I don't want to live surrounded by ghosts. I won't do it.' She stroked the cat at kissed his head.

'Very sensible. You should move closer to me,' Francesca said, huffing as she dragged a suitcase across the room.

'No,' Veronica said steadily. 'I am going to go live by the sea.'

'We're not that far from the coast,' Francesca said defensively.

'I know but I have friends round here. I don't want to leave everything behind.'

'You've got nothing left to leave behind,' Francesca said without thinking.

Veronica stared at her sister with disbelief. Even by her standards, that was callous. 'I'll put the house and the business on the market in the New Year and then decide where I want to go. Andrew had one thing right: Dennis did spend too much time in that bloody shop,' she said angrily.

'Oh, I didn't mean it like that.' Francesca half apologised.

'You never do,' Veronica sighed.

'Don't you think you should get the funeral over and done with first?' Francesca said carefully, broaching the subject for the first time.

'I don't even know when they will release him,' Veronica said miserably.

'I'm sure they'll let you know soon enough,' Francesca said cheerily. 'Have you decided if you want a burial or cremation?'

'Not really. I don't see that it makes any difference. He's gone.'

'Well, personally, I think you should consider cremation. Then you can take him with you wherever you go. Especially since you're considering moving.'

'I'm not considering it, I've made my mind up,' Veronica said forcefully.

'There you are then.' Francesca hooked her handbag over her shoulder.

'I'm going to take Cookie over to Peggy's house. The taxi should be here soon.' She held the cat in her right hand and picked up a bag with a litter tray, a bowl and cat food with her left. She nuzzled her face into Cookie's fur while the feline purred loudly, her tears soaking into the hairs. 'It's time to say goodbye.'

Chapter 22

When Barrett and Palmer arrived outside the Kilpatrick residence in Fulbourn the sky above was angry. Dark storm clouds had gathered above and the birds were flying in all directions warning of the downpour to come.

Palmer pulled his collar up as Barrett knocked on the front door impatiently, which Palmer struggled to understand given that they were there to deliver distressing news.

'Hello?' Susan Kilpatrick peered through a crack in the door.

'DCI Barrett.' He held his badge up.

'Come in,' she said apologetically and stepped aside.

'Thank you.' Palmer smiled politely. 'Would you like us to take our shoes off?' he asked noticing she was wearing slippers.

'If you don't mind.' Everything she said was tinged with embarrassment and concern.

'Of course,' Palmer said slipping his brogues off his feet. Barrett followed suit having already trampled slush into the carpet in the hallway.

'Please come through.' Susan led them into the kitchen. As they passed the living room both inspectors noticed the television was on and a young woman was sat curled up on a sofa. She didn't acknowledge the police and seemed to be in a world of her own.

'My daughter,' Susan explained shutting the kitchen door so that they wouldn't be disturbed. 'Is there any news?'

'There has been a development,' Barrett admitted before pausing. How was he going to tell this woman that her husband's finger had been removed and sent to a local journalist?

'I think it would be best if you took a seat,' Palmer said kindly, sitting down himself and leaving her no option.

'What is it?' she asked, her eyes wide and glassy.

'Yesterday morning a package was delivered to the editor of the *Cambridge News*,' Barrett said steadily.

'Yes, I saw it on the news. The fingers in the box.' Susan turned to Barrett not yet realising the link.

'Two of the fingers belonged to the recent murder victims. The third...' He cleared his throat wishing he had a glass of water. 'We've matched to your husband.'

Susan sat still, blinking and looking from Palmer to Barrett.

'Eddie?' The words came out in a half whisper.

'The DNA matches the DNA from the toothbrush you gave us.'

'Eddie?' she said again in the same high pitch.

'Yes. We are extremely concerned for his safety.' Palmer lent forward.

'Eddie's finger,' she said to herself trying to process the information.

'We are doing everything we can to find him, Mrs Kilpatrick, but now we know Eddie has been targeted by the man responsible for the deaths of two other victims, we really need to find a link. Is there anything you can tell us that might shed some light?' Barrett asked hopefully.

'Is he dead?' She turned to Palmer ignoring Barrett's question.

'We are working on the assumption that he is alive.'

'Mrs Kilpatrick. Barrett moved his chair closer to her. 'We need to know if your husband knew either of the deceased. Do the names Dennis Wade or Wendy Matlock mean anything to you?'

'Dennis?' Her gaze remained fixed on Palmer. 'My husband used to play golf with a man named Dennis.'

'Do you remember his surname?' Barrett asked urgently.

'I'm not sure I ever knew it.' She looked down at her hands, her eyes resting on her splayed fingers.

'What about Wendy Matlock? Does that name ring a bell?' Palmer encouraged.

'No. I've never heard of her.' Susan's voice was fractured.

'Mum?' The young woman who had been sitting on the sofa appeared in the doorway looking concerned. She was wearing a baggy sweatshirt and leggings. Her hair was pulled up in a scruffy bun and she had a tattoo running down her neck. 'What's the matter?'

'DI Palmer,' he said getting up and shaking her hand.

'What's happened?' She stared at him with the same fear on her face as her mother had.

Palmer looked at Susan, not feeling it was his place to tell the woman what had happened, and watched as the mother beckoned for her daughter to come and sit by her side. Palmer could see now that the woman was much older than he had first thought. From a distance she appeared to be in her twenties but on closer inspection it was clear that she was closer to forty. He noticed there was no wedding ring.

'Tell me.' The tattooed woman said, placing her hand on her mother's shoulder.

Barrett and Palmer were quiet while Susan told her daughter the news.

'So he's dead?' The woman turned to Barrett with a look of horror on her face.

'We don't believe so.' Barrett tried to focus on her face rather than the large floral tattoo that snaked up the left side of her neck.

'Do you know a Wendy Matlock or Dennis Wade?' Palmer asked.

'No, sorry.' She blinked back tears trying to be strong for her mother who sat completely still and ghost-like.

'Dad used to play golf with a Dennis, didn't he?' Susan said to the woman who still hadn't been properly introduced to the policemen.

'Yes, I think you're right.' The woman nodded as a strand of hair freed itself from her bun. 'He did have a golf buddy called Dennis a while back. Not heard him mention him for years though.' She spoke with a slight lisp due to the fact she had a rather large tongue piercing.

Palmer struggled to see how Susan could be the woman's mother. Although they shared similar features, Susan was dowdy in her appearance and her daughter was the opposite.

'I'm sorry, I didn't catch your name,' Barrett cut in.

'I'm Marie.' Her eyes were fixed on her mother's face.

'Is there any way you might be able to find out Dennis's surname?'

'Dad's old diaries!' Marie said all of a sudden. 'He's very particular and keeps all his old diaries. It will take a while to find the right one but if his surname is anywhere, it will be in there. Where are they, Mum?' she said turning to look at her mother who had returned to staring down at her fingers.

'In a box. In the attic,' she said vaguely.

'Why is this person cutting people's fingers off?' Susan looked up at Palmer.

'We don't know yet.' It pained him to admit it.

'Would you like me to go up into the attic?' Barrett asked standing up.

'No, I'll do it later.' Marie looked at him with distrust.

'We need that name as soon as possible. I would rather take the diaries with me now so that my team can start going through them.'

'You're not taking them.' She half laughed. 'They don't belong to you. I'll look through them and let you know when I find the name.'

'I'm sorry if you think I am being pushy, but your father is in serious danger. We don't have time to spare.'

'You can have them,' Susan told him resting her hand on her daughter's arm and squeezing it. 'We just want him back.'

'Thank you, Mrs Kilpatrick.'

'There is a ladder in the garden shed. Somewhere in the attic you'll find a box which has diaries written on it in large letters.'

Barrett nodded and headed out of the back door and into the garden to retrieve the ladder just as the rain started to pour. He'd forgotten he had taken his shoes off and returned with soaking wet socks and a look of irritation. If the situation hadn't been so grave, Palmer might have laughed.

After manoeuvring the ladder through the kitchen and up the stairs Barrett found himself poking about in a large dark attic. It was the most ordered attic he had ever been in and it didn't take long to identify the box Susan told him about.

Once back downstairs, Barrett put his wet feet into his shoes, after thanking Susan and Marie for their time and cooperation, before heading back out into the downpour followed closely by Palmer.

'She's as character,' Palmer said referring to Marie and wiping the raindrops from his face.

'Call Hale and Singh,' Barrett barked as he started the engine. 'I want them waiting at the station ready to go through these diaries. Everything else can be put on hold.'

***

Roy Dunlop had been waiting for the rain to pass before he ventured out to walk his golden Labrador. The dog, Marlow, had been scratching at the front door and dropping heavy hints all afternoon so, when the downpour finally ceased, Roy pulled on his Barbour jacket and flat cap and grabbed the dog's lead.

Closing the door on his cottage he wondered why he'd given in. An icy wind was blowing and darkness was already falling.

He walked along Toyse Lane on the outskirts of Burwell and kept his head down, wanting to avoid the drizzle. Marlow pulled hard on the lead and tugged his master along the lane, making Roy move at a faster pace than he wished to. It was his wife who insisted they had a dog, yet he was the one tasked with walking the creature. Still, he knew when he got home that a nice steak and onion pie would be waiting so it wasn't all bad.

It was the same walk he did every day, along Toyse Lane and right onto North Street before heading up Little Fen Drove. He walked along the quiet country track, avoiding puddles, before turning onto the footpath that led to the fishing lakes and letting

Marlow run free. The dog immediately went galloping through the deep muddy puddles enjoying his freedom and not giving a second thought to the fact that he would have to be bathed when he got home.

Roy plodded along behind, his gumboots squelching in the thick mud. From his pocket he removed a small torch so that he could see in the gloom. The drizzle had relented but the sky was still heavy with dark clouds.

As he reached the edge of a lake he stopped to see where Marlow was. The dog was on the other side of the water barking at a tree. Rolling his eyes, Roy made his way round the perimeter to see what the dog was making a fuss about. He wasn't prepared for the body he discovered hanging from one of the branches.

The skull had been caved in and the torso was a bloody mess, the clothes ripped revealing skin and wounds. Below the corpse, the dog went on barking, its hackles up while its feet stood in a puddle of rainwater marbled with blood.

Chapter 23

5.50pm Sunday 22nd December

'Get hold of Bob. We need SOCOs at the scene immediately.' Barrett pulled on his overcoat while talking at Elly, who was working her way through Eddie Kilpatrick's diaries.

'Palmer, we're going to Burwell,' he called across the room his voice cracking with exhaustion.

'Burwell?' Palmer looked up from his desk, the screen reflected in his eyes.

'Yes, we have another one.'

'Eddie Kilpatrick?'

'That would be my guess.' Barrett buttoned up his coat and ran his hand through his silver hair. 'A body was found by a dog walker. It doesn't sound like it's in a pretty state. Unlike our previous victims this one had been hung from a tree by a fishing lake on the outskirts of the village.'

'Not a suicide?' Palmer asked, thinking about Susan and Marie.

'Doesn't sound like it.' Barrett shook his head. 'Let's go.'

Palmer grabbed the half-eaten baguette that was sitting on his desk and followed his colleague out of the room. He always had an increased appetite in the winter.

'Any other information?'

'The victim is male. In his sixties or seventies. Hung by the neck. There is blood at the scene. That's all I know until we get there.'

'Sounds like our man,' Palmer admitted as his heart sank.

With a new murder to add to the investigation, it was looking increasingly likely that he would not be spending Christmas day at home as planned.

The men drove to Burwell in silence, once they'd finally got away from the crawling winter traffic. The dark roads that led to the scene where the body had been discovered were eerily abandoned and the car bumped along the rough surface, its headlights on full beam. But there was very little to see. The fields around there were flat and the darkness seemed to go on forever.

Followed closely by two police cars it took them half an hour to reach their destination.

When they pulled onto Little Fen Drove, they spotted a man standing by a large metal gate on the edge of the lane. He looked cold. By his feet sat a Labrador covered in mud.

'Over here.' He waved the police down as Barrett pulled onto the kerb. 'It's over here.' Roy stood shivering in the cold. Barrett suspected he had shock.

After pulling on shoe protectors and gloves the inspectors and the officers followed the man through the near darkness to the edge of the lake.

'I'm not going any further. I've seen enough.' The man stopped, trying to control the dog, which pulled hard on the lead. 'Go round that way.' He pointed left. 'Keep to the edge of the lake and you'll find it soon enough.'

'Thank you.' Barrett nodded and set off leaving Palmer to tell Roy he should go back to the lane and get himself checked out by the ambulance. Roy, who was only too happy to put as much distance between himself and the dead body, agreed and returned to their meeting spot. The rain was beginning to fall again.

It took the inspectors a few minutes before they found what they were looking for. Barrett stopped, holding his torch up and lighting the scene. It was something out of a nightmare.

'Jesus,' Palmer whispered under his breath when he caught up with his boss.

Stepping closer only made it more real. The head of the victim was caved in on one side, pieces of smashed bone sticking out of the skull in peculiar angles. The smallest finger on the right hand had been removed and the chest was a bloody mess of cut flesh.

The victim's eyes were bulging and bloodshot, staring out over the lake.

'Have you ever seen anything like this before?' Palmer asked Barrett.

'I can honestly say in all my years on the force this is the first time I've encountered anything like this.' His words were tainted with horror and morbid fascination.

'He looks like he's been here a while.'

'Agreed,' Barrett said, carefully stepping closer to the corpse and shining the light on the chest. 'Get them to cordon off the area. I don't want anyone else disturbing the scene.'

'The rain will have washed away a lot.'

'But we need to salvage what we can, Joe.' Barrett didn't want to acknowledge the fact that so much evidence would have been lost.

Grateful to be leaving the corpse, Palmer returned to the officers who were making their way along the path and gave them their instructions, just as Bob Roland and his team joined them.

'Evening,' Bob said through his surgical mask. 'What do we have here?'

'Looking like The Hangman has struck again.'

'Righto. Didn't take him long.' Bob snapped his nitrile gloves on and followed the path around the lake to join Barrett who stayed with the body.

'Ian.' The men shook hands. 'Any idea who this might be?'

'It's Eddie Kilpatrick. He went missing two days ago.' Although the body hanging from the tree looked far from human, Barrett knew the man had once been Eddie.

'Any links to the previous victims?' Bob asked.

'That's what we are trying to establish.' Barrett watched as Bob slowly circled the body being careful not to step in the bloody puddle below it. 'What is it?' he asked, finally acknowledging the strange look on Bob's face.

'See here?' Bob pointed with a gloved finger. 'These cuts. They don't look random. I think something has been carved into the skin.'

Barrett took a tentative step towards the body and cocked his head. Bob was right. It looked like letters.

'I won't be sure until I get it back to the lab and get him cleaned up,' Bob admitted, now examining the stump where the small finger had once been. 'You don't need me to tell you, but this is different to the others.'

'Our killer seems to be getting more violent.'

'Yes,' Bob said gravely 'and more confident.'

'I'm going to leave you to it,' sighed Barrett. 'I need to go and break the news to his family.'

'Rather you than me,' Bob said puffing out his cheeks. 'I'm more comfortable dealing with the dead. They don't cry.'

'No, they don't.' He looked up at the glassy bloated expression on the victim's face and felt a real sense of sadness.

Had Eddie Kilpatrick begged for his life? Did he know the end was coming? Pushing away the questions that were trying to get into his head he made his way back along the edge of the lake leaving Bob and his team to work the scene.

'Time to break the news to Mrs Kilpatrick,' he said to Palmer who was chatting to one of the uniformed officers. 'I didn't think we'd be visiting her again today.'

'No, neither did I.' Palmer played with the house keys that were in his pocket just as his mobile phone began to ring. Elly Hale's name appeared on his screen.

'Hello, yes?'

'I've been going through the diaries. I've found a name. Dennis Wade appears on a number of occasions in the calendar from 1995 through to 1999. Then there is no mention of him again. It's odd. Most of the entries which have Dennis Wade also have the word golf written next to them, but there are couple of time when the name appears on its own.'

'I want you to write a list of dates when the name appears and email it over to me.' Palmer put his hand up to stop Barrett who was about to interrupt. 'We've found Eddie Kilpatrick and we are on our way to break the news to his family now.'

'Oh dear.' Elly sounded genuinely upset.

'We'll speak to the family and then come back to the station. Prepare yourself for a long night and tell the others, too.'

'Will do. Are you alright?'

'I'm fine,' Palmer replied defensively. It was not the sort of personal question he was comfortable with. 'We'll see you soon.' He hung up.

'Elly has confirmed that Dennis Wade's name appears in a number of the diaries.' Palmer filled Barrett in on the conversation.

'Let's get over there and arrange for a FLO to meet us outside. That family are going to need all the support they can get.'

'At least they don't have to ID the body.' Palmer was grasping around for a silver lining.

'Yes. At least we can spare them that.'

Twenty-five minutes later they were standing outside 79 Bridewell Road in Fulbourn. Through the window they could see the Christmas tree lights glowing. On the front door hung an artificial ivy wreath adorned with fake red berries.

Palmer took a deep breath before knocking on the door. The cold air filled his lungs making them ache for a moment.

Marie answered the door. She was now wearing a pair of checked green flannel pyjamas. She looked like a great big kid and it was endearing.

'Can we come in?' Palmer said as she stood looking at them.

'Is it the diaries? Have you found something?'

'It would be better if we could do this indoors,' Barrett suggested, but Marie stood in the doorway blocking their path; she knew they were not bringing good news.

'Okay.' She finally moved aside and let the officers in.

Without having to ask, Palmer and Barrett both slipped their shoes off before following her into the living room.

Slouched on the sofa was Susan, cradling a glass of dark liquor. 'I wasn't expecting guests.' Susan sat up, half slurring.

'She's had a few.' Marie nodded at the bottle of Tia Maria on the table. 'I thought it would help her sleep.'

'Sorry for disturbing you again,' Palmer apologised looking at Barrett – wanting him to take the lead.

'What it is?' Susan's eyes were not focusing on any of their faces.

'Earlier this evening…' Barrett stepped forward. 'We received a call reporting a body.'

Marie held her breath, knowing what was coming but not wanting to hear it.

'I'm afraid the body belonged to Mr Kilpatrick,' Barrett said staring at the pile of presents already placed under the Christmas tree. He wondered how many of them were meant for a man who would never open them.

'No.' Susan blinked. 'No. You're wrong.'

Marie collapsed onto the sofa next to her mother and hugged her, burying her face in her shoulder to hide the tears.

'You're wrong,' Susan said again.

'I'm really sorry, Mrs Kilpatrick, but we've formally identified the victim as your husband. We are very sorry for your loss.'

'I'm Julie,' said the family liaison officer who bent down on her haunches. 'I'm here to help you.' Her face was kind and she looked older than she was. Dealing with victim's families time and time again had taken its toll on her and the crow's feet around her eyes were deep set.

Susan stared blankly at her as Marie's sobs grew louder and she began repeating the word 'Dad' over and over again.

'What happened to him?' Susan finally managed to ask.

'He was murdered.' Barrett delivered the next blow.

'Where is he?' Marie asked looking up at last.

'The body was discovered outside of Burwell by a fishing lake. Does that mean anything to you?'

Both women shook their heads in tandem.

'I appreciate this is a shock, but I have just one more question. We've discovered that your husband did know Dennis Wade. His name appears in your father's diaries.' Barrett addressed only Marie since Susan seemed incapable of talking or thinking straight. 'Can you tell us anything about their relationship?'

Wiping away the large tears that were falling down her face Marie paused for a moment and thought. 'They played golf sometimes a while back. I'd not heard Dad mention him for years.'

'Do you know how they met?'

'Maybe through the golf club.'

'Which club is that?' Palmer asked removing his notepad.

'The Gog Magog Golf club,' Susan said with no emotion.

'Thank you.' Palmer smiled kindly. 'We are going to leave you with Julie now. Again, we are very sorry not to be delivering better news.'

***

By midnight the incident room had quietened down. The officers were all seated at their own desks working on the new case and filing reports.

Barrett sat alone in his office going over things in his mind. Since discovering a link between Dennis and Eddie he was sure that Wendy also knew the other victims. It was possible she too was a member of the golf club. He remembered seeing all of her activity photographs on the wall in her house, but he didn't recall seeing any evidence of golf.

Picking up the phone he called the mortuary. 'Can I speak to Bob Roland please. DCI Barrett here.' He closed his eyes and rubbed his right temple with his free hand. After a moment Bob came to the phone.

'Ian.' He cleared his throat.

'Can you tell me if there were any golf clubs at Wendy Matlock's house?'

'Not that I recall,' Bob replied. He found the question strange.

'It seems we can link Eddie Kilpatrick to Dennis Wade through a golf club and I wondered if that was also the link to Wendy Matlock.' He sighed with exhaustion.

'Not as far as I remember, but I can check the scene of crime photographs and come back to you on that.' He paused for a moment. 'You sound tired.'

'I am,' Barrett admitted before he could stop himself. It wasn't like him to confess to such a thing.

'You should go home. Get some sleep. This will still be here in the morning.'

'Sleep?' Barrett chuckled. 'Do you sleep well when working an active case?'

'I've learnt to.'

'Lucky for some.'

'How were the family?' Bob thought he already knew the answer to this question but felt compelled to ask.

'Awful,' came the simple reply.

'Nasty business,' he said looking down at the dirty overalls he had on. 'Anyway, I thought you'd want to know that I was right about the torso. A message was cut into the body.'

'Message? What message?' Barrett sat upright suddenly feeling wide awake.

'It goes some way to explaining why the small right-hand fingers were removed from each victim,' Bob continued dangling the carrot.

'What does?'

'Once I caught a fish alive.'

'You mean like the nursery rhyme?' Barrett said frowning and scratching his head.

'Exactly. The letters were carved using some sort of sharp instrument, most likely a knife.'

'Okay.' Barrett's brain was whirling again.

'I'd say the victim was killed late on Friday. He'd been hanging there for some time. Rigor mortis had set in.'

Barrett nodded jotting all this down. 'Thanks for letting me know.'

'You'll have my report in the morning.' Bob yawned. 'Oh, and one last thing. He was alive when the words were cut into him.'

***

In Fulbourn, Susan sat upstairs in her bed surrounded by all of Eddie's remaining diaries. Flicking through the pages, looking at his handwriting and remembering days gone by, she struggled to focus on the words. The sleeping pill Marie had given her was clashing with the alcohol she'd consumed.

Downstairs below her she could hear her daughter pacing the living room and crying.

Numb from the medication and booze, Susan was determined to keep going through the diaries nonetheless. She didn't know if she was looking for anything in particular but having them with her made her feel closer to her murdered husband.

Opening a diary that was from 1983 she came across initials she didn't recognise. Scribbled on every Monday for over six months were the letters GM, then, all of a sudden, the initials stopped appearing.

Susan searched for the diary he'd kept in eighty-four and scoured the pages for those same initials, but they were nowhere to be seen. Then, in a bizarre moment of clarity, perhaps brought on by the multiple substances swirling around her system, Susan remembered that was the year she realised Eddie was having an affair; and she suspected GM was the woman in question. Susan let out a long sigh and let the diary fall to the floor. The identity of the woman in question was no longer relevant, but she still needed to know. In the morning she'd ask Marie if she had any idea who GM was.

Lying back on her bed, her head sinking into the pillow, she thought back to those days. She'd been so cross, so hurt by Eddie's betrayal, and in that moment those feelings came flooding back. For the first time since she'd been put to bed by her daughter, Susan finally let herself cry.

Chapter 24

Marie sat on the sofa staring at the television, which wasn't on. Upstairs, her mother was asleep in bed having taken a heavy dose of sleeping tablets.

Only the Christmas tree lights were on creating a soft glow in the living room, which was otherwise gloomy.

In her hands she held onto one of her father's jumpers. It still smelt of his cologne. She'd removed it from the laundry basket after her mother had fallen asleep. Marie had not slept a wink. She sat up the whole night crying. She had decided against taking the sleeping pills she'd plied her mother with. She couldn't handle both their pain at once. She needed time to process some of her own before she dealt with anyone else's grief.

For hours she'd tried hard to remember anything about Dennis Wade. She knew she'd never met him, but she wondered if there was some other detail she had that would help the police catch the animal responsible for her dad's murder.

Marie had a sudden urge to leave. She wanted to get away from the house she'd grown up in and return to London. Maybe there her reality would be different. Maybe there she could avoid thinking about his death. But Marie knew she had to stay. Her mother needed her. They needed each other. She couldn't escape this, no matter how far she went it would always be there.

Last night, after the police had left, Susan had retrieved the vacuum cleaner from the cupboard under the stairs and had proceeded to vacuum the living room, complaining about the number of needles the Christmas tree had dropped on the carpet.

Marie couldn't see any needles but didn't try to stop her mother. The FLO had explained that it was common for people to start cleaning moments after receiving terrible news of that magnitude. It was people's way of controlling their surroundings when they felt otherwise helpless. Marie understood it made vague sense, but she'd been unable to sit there and watch her mother vacuum and had taken herself into the bathroom to run a hot shower, hoping the noise of the water would drown out her loud guttural cries.

Folding her father's jumper neatly and setting it down to one side, Marie stood up and moved over to the Christmas tree. On the top was a fairy that her mother had used every year for as long as she could remember. Marie cradled a small glass decoration that hung from one of the branches, remembering happy times in her childhood and Christmases spent with her father. Every year he'd dressed up as Father Christmas and volunteered at the school fair.

Removing the decoration from the branch she let it go, watching it fall to the ground, where it smashed into lots of tiny pieces. Some of the splinters just missed her feet. Next, she reached up and took the angel off the top of the tree before pulling it apart and throwing the remains on the floor. It felt good letting go and before she realised what she was doing she'd lifted the entire tree and hurled it across the room. It went crashing into a wall, knocking a picture of her father and mother together down and breaking the frame.

Scrabbling over the chaotic scene of broken branches and decorations, Marie ended up on her knees holding the damaged picture.

'I'm sorry,' she sobbed clutching the photo to her chest and ignoring the bleeding cuts on her hands. 'I'm so, so, sorry.'

***

Palmer drove the car while Elly sat quietly in the passenger seat. The pair were on their way to The Gog Magog Golf Course to talk to the staff about Dennis and Eddie. As usual, the Christmas traffic was almost at a standstill.

They pulled up outside the clubhouse and stepped out into the bitter wind. Elly tugged her coat tight around her body and tucked her face into her collar.

At reception a spotty young man, who looked at them nervously as Palmer got out his badge, greeted them.

'We'd like to speak to the manager, please.' Elly smiled, wanting to alleviate his fears.

'That'd be Mr Boyd,' he said. 'Is he expecting you?'

'No. But we need to speak him. Is he here?'

'Should be.' The teenager shrugged.

'Where?' Palmer's patience was wearing thin.

'I'll go get him for you.' The young man sloped off leaving the desk unattended.

'Not exactly busy, is it,' Elly said looking around.

'Boring game if you ask me,' Palmer lent over and whispered.

'I can't imagine you playing golf.' She giggled.

'I don't but if I did, I'm sure I'd be good.' He winked.

'Can I help you?' A fat man in a brown suit appeared with the boy.

'DI Palmer and this is Sergeant Hale.' Palmer shook his hand. 'Is there somewhere private we can talk?'

'Tim Boyd.' He had a sweaty palm. 'Follow me,' the manager said leading them up some stairs and into the main clubhouse room, which had a bar and views out over the golf course. Taking them to a table with armchairs on the far side of the room, Tim sat down and beckoned for them to do the same. 'Joan won't interrupt us.' He pointed over to the woman who stood behind the bar. His breathing was heavy. Clearly the stairs had taken it out of him.

'Thank you for agreeing to talk to us. This is a delicate matter which involves some club members.'

'Oh?' The fat man raised an eyebrow and dabbed his brow.

'Yes. We'd like to talk to you about Dennis Wade and Edward Kilpatrick. Are you familiar with those names?'

'I am.' He was pompous in his response and Palmer took an instant dislike to him.

'Are both men members?'

'Dennis has been coming to the club for years, but he's a fair-weather golfer. Only comes in the spring and summer months.' Palmer wondered if Tim Boyd knew that Dennis Wade had been killed.

'And Edward Kilpatrick?'

'Now there is a blast from the past.' Tim wiped his forehead again. 'A name I've not heard for a while. He used to be a member, back in the nineties. A regular, he was, but then he just stopped playing and one year didn't renew his membership. I pride myself on knowing all our customers.' His smugness was leaking out of his skin.

'But Mr Wade remains a member?'

'Well, he was until someone sent him up to heaven,' Tim said turning red in the face. Palmer sat there stunned. This man had no idea how to conduct himself. 'Can I get you a tea or coffee?' Tim turned to face Joan, his chair squeaking below his heavy frame.

'Not for me.' Palmer didn't want to extend the interview any longer than necessary.

'Tea would be lovely,' Elly replied, much to Palmer's frustration.

'Two teas, Joan,' Tim called across the room. 'Now where were we…'

'Dennis Wade,' Palmer said flatly.

'Ah yes. It's been quite the talk of the club.' Tim's beady little eyes shone in his face. 'It's not everyday someone you know is murdered.'

'Did you know him well?' Elly asked.

'We'd have a chat from time to time, but I can't say I knew him exactly. He seemed like a nice sort. He was good with all his volunteering and helpful to the community.'

'Volunteering?' Palmer's ears pricked up.

'Yes, you know. His charity work, the scouts and all that.'

'Scouts?'

Tim frowned at Palmer, irritated that he was being mirrored. 'Yes, for a time I believe Dennis was a scout leader.'

'I see.' Palmer jotted this down on his pad. 'And what about his relationship with Edward Kilpatrick?'

'Eddie and Dennis would often play golf together. I think they met through the club but I can't be certain.' A bead of sweat travelled slowly down the side of Tim's face. 'One day Eddie just stopped coming. I'm not one to pry.'

Palmer doubted that was true. 'Do you have any club records anywhere?'

'Of course we do,' he snarled just as Joan appeared carrying a tray with two cups on it.

'I'll need to see those.' Palmer stared at him coldly.

'What about Wendy Matlock? Does that name sound familiar?' Elly asked.

'No.' Tim took his cup off the tray.

'I knew Wendy,' Joan suddenly said out of nowhere. The three people sat at the table looked up at her with disbelief. 'Although that was when she was Wendy Connor, before she married. She worked here for a few summers when she left school. Lovely girl she was. So polite.'

'When was that?' Palmer's pen hovered over his note pad.

'Now let me see…' Joan stood leaning on her hip and cocked her head to one side while searching her memory. 'Must have been around ninety-six, ninety-seven, something like that. She worked in the kitchen as a pot washer.'

Palmer nodded wanting to encourage her. This was the link they'd been looking for. He'd never have guessed it would have come from this unassuming bartender.

'I can't say for certain, but I think it was around then. There'll be records of her employment somewhere in the system, I imagine,' Joan said turning to Tim, who was looking at her with rage.

'We've had lots of temps come and go over the years. I can't be expected to remember all their damn names.' It was clear to Palmer and Elly that he hadn't been trying to hide anything, he'd simply forgotten, and given that over twenty years had passed it wasn't that surprising.

Palmer sat back in his chair and folded his arms across his chest. Rather than dislike Tim he decided, in fact, that he felt sorry for him. What sort of man remains in the same dead-end job for over twenty years? It was obvious that Tim Boyd was happy being a big fish in a small pond and Palmer wondered if there would ever be room for any other fish at all.

'We'll need to see employment records and anything else you have relating to Wendy Matlock – or Wendy Connor, as she was then – Dennis Wade or Eddie Kilpatrick.'

'I think I've made it clear that I'm happy to assist you.' Tim straightened in his seat, his large belly resting on his thighs.

'I'll need to take your name and contact details, please, Joan?' Elly requested.

'Sure thing, love.' Joan nodded and smiled revealing tobacco stained teeth.

She looked like a badly-aged silver service waitress with her white shirt and black trousers. Elly found herself wondering if Joan had worked at the golf club as long as Tim Boyd had.

'Can you tell us if there were ever any issues at the club? Any arguments? Did Wendy, Dennis or Eddie ever fall out with anyone?'

'Why are you asking about Eddie?' Tim suddenly said narrowing his eyes.

'I'm not at liberty to divulge that information at this time.' Palmer brushed some imaginary fluff off his trousers casually.

'Three fingers. Three bodies,' the large man said to himself hoisting his weight up out of the seat. 'You can count on my discretion.'

'It would be wise to keep your suspicions to yourself, Mr Boyd. You wouldn't want to jeopardise or interfere with an on-going case, now, would you?' Palmer retorted with a sarcastic grin before taking down Joan's details and leaving the clubhouse with Elly in tow.

***

Tilly sat in her bed, wrapped in her crumpled-up sheets, hugging her knees. The basement flat was cold although the heating was on. On the other side of her bedroom door she could hear Yuki moving around in the living room. The television was loud and Tilly listened to the morning news.

'Another victim of The Hangman was discovered in Burwell late last night by a man walking his dog. The body of man, who has yet to be named, was found hanging from a tree next to Burwell Fishing Lakes. The authorities are on the scene and have cordoned off the area. Anyone who saw anything suspicious is encouraged to contact the police or Crimestoppers.

'This is the third murder in ten days and police appear to be no nearer to identifying the person responsible. Cambridgeshire residents have been urged to be vigilant.

'In other news…'

At that point Tilly lay down in bed and put her pillow over her head. She'd heard more than she wanted to. She was scared enough when the second body was discovered but now, she was terrified.

Although the police had given her permission to return to Devon she felt compelled to stay until the case was wrapped up. Tilly didn't know if it would be weeks or months, but she knew that if she went back to Ilfracombe she'd never return to Cambridge. She had to see this out, even if it meant staying in that grotty flat for Christmas, even if it meant not seeing her family, because she was petrified and she was sick of feeling that way. Her entire life Tilly had been brave and this new fear she felt made her question who she was. Determined to have the life she wanted and to finish her veterinary training, Tilly was adamant that she had to face her fear. She'd never run away from anything before and she was not about to change the habit of a lifetime, even if it put her mental health under threat.

She lay in bed wondering about the identity of the third victim. The newsreader had said it was male, so she knew that much but nothing more. Tilly suspected it wouldn't take long for his name to be released and knew that even when it was it probably wouldn't make a difference to her. She just hoped he was a stranger, unlike Dennis, her boss.

Suddenly she had an urge to see the other employees from the shop. She realised she needed to get out, to walk the streets of Cambridge and face her fear. The only people in the world who knew what she was going through were her colleagues. Reaching a hand out from below her duvet she felt about on her bedside table for her mobile phone and dialled Jane.

The phone rang for quite some time before Jane finally answered.

'Yes.' Her voice was clipped.

'Hello, Jane. It's Tilly,' she said in a childlike tone.

'I know. Your name came up.'

'Oh, yes, right. I just wondered if we could get together and meet for a drink perhaps?'

'You weren't at our last meeting.' Jane's words were unforgiving.

'I know. I've been struggling but I'd like to see you.' She paused. 'And the others.'

'You've heard there has been a third, I assume?'

'Yes.' Tilly shivered beneath the covers.

'It's quite unacceptable.' Jane ran her hand through her wild hair. 'I don't know what the police are actually doing.'

'Can we meet?' There was pleading in Tilly's voice.

'Where and when?'

'I don't mind.' She hadn't thought that far ahead. 'Maybe I should call the others and see what suits everyone best,' she suggested.

'Well why don't you call me and tell me when you've decided. I'll let you know if I can make it, depending on my schedule.' Jane always did like to make herself seem more important and busier than she was.

'Okay. I'll speak to the others and come back to you.' Tilly felt small.

'Perhaps don't bother to invite Marcus,' Jane said carefully. 'He's not really one of us anyway.'

'Alright,' Tilly agreed but did not know why she'd done so. 'I'll be in touch later on today. Thanks, Jane,' she said as the line went dead.

Having not enjoyed that phone call one bit, Tilly decided it would be better to text the others instead.

An hour later she had only managed to get Steven to agree to meet. There had always been a mild attraction between them and she was pleased she would get to see his face the following lunchtime. Steven had suggested they meet at The Fort St George pub which was on the river. It was a cosy pub with low ceilings, wooden beams and a large fireplace, and Tilly agreed it would be a good spot for a drink and a bite to eat.

Not wanting to talk to Jane again she texted her the plan: *Meet at Fort St George. 12.30am tomorrow x.*

A few moments later Tilly received a response: *It's too far from me. I will pass.*

Tilly wasn't at all surprised when she felt relieved. A nice lunch with Steven and a bit of harmless flirting was just what the doctor ordered.

Throwing back the covers she got out of bed and went to join Yuki in the living room, feeling better than she had done for days.

'You better?' Yuki asked putting her phone aside for a moment. 'You look better.'

'I'm doing okay.' Tilly even managed a small smile.

'I still fink you go home.' Yuki frowned. 'Need family now. Not Yuki.'

'You're very sweet and I appreciate your concern, but I have to stay. At least for a little while.'

'Family come here?' Yuki asked.

'They said they might, but they had everything planned for Christmas at home. I told them I'd be fine and we could catch up in the New Year. I don't want to ruin their plans.'

'More body.' Yuki pointed at the television, which was on mute. 'Man found by lake.'

'Yes, I know,' Tilly said quietly.

'Yuki no like Cambridge now. Yuki think China better.' She smiled.

'Are you leaving?' Tilly was shocked.

'No. But me no go out alone. Not safe.' She waggled her finger. 'Not at night. Not in day.'

'Are you frightened?' Tilly sat down next to her flatmate and crossed her legs beneath her.

'Yes. You?' Yuki tucked her dark hair behind her ears.

'Terrified.' Tilly smiled weakly.

'Good. Scared good. Brave, silly. You stay with Yuki. We be safe.'

The women hugged, and Tilly felt grateful that she had Yuki in her life.

***

Barrett stood in front of his team in the incident room and held court. 'Good morning, everyone. I know we're all tired, but I'd appreciate your attention.

'Yesterday evening the body of Mr Edward Kilpatrick was discovered by Burwell Fishing Lake. Just like the first two victims the little finger on his right hand had been removed. Not only that, but the lyric of a children's nursery rhyme was cut into his chest.'

Barrett turned to face the whiteboard behind him and wrote the words, 'once I caught a fish alive' in red pen.

'We now have a partial understanding of the relevance of removing the fingers. The fact that Mr Kilpatrick was murdered next to a fishing lake must also mean something to our killer.

'As of yesterday evening, we have established that Dennis Wade and Edward Kilpatrick were acquaintances. Also, this morning, DI Palmer learned that Wendy Matlock worked at the golf course where the men played golf together.

'We've been through the victims' history and there doesn't appear to be a particular link to fishing. The link is the golf club.

'While interviewing the golf club manager, DI Palmer learned a few more things regarding Dennis Wade's past, which he is going to look into.

'I want the rest of you to search for evidence that Wendy Matlock and Eddie Kilpatrick fished. I want you.' He pointed at Singh. 'To go through the nursery rhyme and see if you can find anything else that might be relevant.

'I don't have to tell you people that tomorrow is Christmas Eve. Let's work hard to focus on the case. We're closing in on our perpetrator. Let's not let him slip through the cracks. We have three families desperate for answers and justice. Let's deliver it to them.'

Around the room people nodded and returned to their desks as Barrett approached Palmer. 'Joe, we need to speak to Mrs Wade. Can I leave that with you?'

'I'm already on the case, sir.' Palmer saluted. 'She's gone to her sister's in Somerset but I've scheduled a call for later this morning.'

'Good work. I'm waiting on the post-mortem results from the coroner to come in.' Barrett checked his watch impatiently. 'We've made good progress. Let's keep it up.'

Chapter 25

Veronica sat on the edge of her bed waiting for the phone to ring. She'd been about to go to church with her sister when Palmer had called to say he needed to ask a few questions. She explained it was a bad time and that she would have to talk to him later. He agreed to call her back after she'd returned from the service.

The spare room at Francesca's house was small. It had once been Natalie's bedroom, but all the posters and her personal belongings had been boxed. The single bed was now made with a floral quilt and the curtains had been replaced to match. Apart from a chair in the corner and a single wardrobe the room was rather bare and unwelcoming.

At 11.37am Veronica's mobile phone rang and she answered almost immediately.

'Mrs Wade,' DI Palmer's calming voice travelled down the line, 'sorry for interrupting earlier. Thank you for agreeing to speak to me now.'

'Have there been any developments?' Her head had been going around in circles ever since he'd first called.

'Actually, there have. I'm sorry to tell you there has been a third victim.'

Veronica hung her head and closed her eyes.

'This information has not been released to the general public yet, but his name was Eddie Kilpatrick. Does that mean anything to you?'

Veronica's eyes sprang open and she nearly fell off the bed.

'I've not heard that name in a very long time.' She felt her stomach turn. 'Yes, he was a member of the golf club Dennis played at in the spring and summer months. They used to play together quite regularly but then Eddie left the club and I'd not heard Dennis mention him since.'

'What about the name Wendy Connor?'

'You mean Matlock?'

'No, I mean Connor. Matlock was her marital name.'

'No, that's not familiar.' Veronica shook her head with certainty.

'Did you ever meet Eddie Kilpatrick?' Palmer asked with interest.

'I never did. They did men's things together. I didn't like going to the golf club much. It wasn't for me.'

'The manager at the club mentioned that Dennis had been involved in the scouts. Is that true?'

'Oh yes. He'd loved it. But that was many years ago now. He stopped volunteering in the late nineties. It was taking up too much of his spare time, he said.'

'Was Andrew ever a scout?'

'We tried.' Veronica let out a long sigh. 'But he didn't like it. He never participated so we gave up making him go. It was a shame. I think it would have done him some good.'

'I see,' said Palmer furiously writing notes.

'Can you tell me which scout troop your husband led?'

'Cambridge, I think. They used to meet once a week at a hall in Chesterton. Occasionally they'd do trips.'

'What sort of trips?'

'Oh, you know, camping, fishing, that sort of thing.'

Palmer stopped dead in his tracks.

'Fishing?'

'Yes. Lots of outdoorsy stuff. Songs round the campfire, canoeing, building dens. The children loved it.'

'So why did Dennis stop then?'

'Well…' Veronica paused for a moment and started to pick a piece of loose cotton from the quilt. 'There was an accident.'

Palmer kept quiet, giving her time to tell the story.

'One of the boys, he… he died.' It was something she hadn't thought about for a long time.

'How?' Palmer encouraged.

'It was so sad. Dennis was distraught,' she said. 'He'd been a member of Dennis's group for a few years. One day his parents came home from work and found him.' She swallowed hard. 'The boy had killed himself.'

'When was this, Mrs Wade?' Palmer's thoughts were whirling.

'Soon before Dennis stopped volunteering. Ninety-eight, I think.'

'Do you know the boy's name?'

'It was Jack, I think. I never met the poor lad. Scouts, like golf, was Dennis's thing.'

'Do you know how he died?'

'I just told you it was suicide.' Her back went rigid. She was not comfortable remembering.

'Is there anything else you think we should know?'

Veronica paused. 'I don't see how any of this is relevant. It was years ago now.'

'Please,' Palmer said gently.

'Dennis was so distraught he couldn't even attend the boy's funeral. It was a difficult time,' Veronica replied softening.

'Okay, Mrs Wade. You've been extremely helpful. We'll be in touch if we have any more questions or if there are any further developments.'

'Thank you,' Veronica said standing and going over to the window to look out over the fields. 'Tell me, before you go, is it still snowing in Cambridge?'

'Erm, no. Not at the moment. We've had rain.' Palmer wondered why they were discussing the weather. 'But the forecast says more snow is due.'

'It's beautiful here,' she said as her eyes filled with tears. 'I hope you have a white Christmas, Inspector.'

'Thank you, Mrs Wade.' He felt himself choking up. 'I hope so too.'

'Make the most of your family,' she said through her tears. 'Every moment is precious.'

'I will. Take care of yourself.' Palmer hung up and sat back in his office chair.

He looked around the incident room at everyone busily working and for a moment had a desire to pick up his computer and hurl it through the window. Most of the time he managed to compartmentalise his emotions from his work but hearing the sadness in her voice brought everything crashing through.

He knew that being a policeman was important. He was helping people and keeping the city safe, but he also knew that these moments with his son would come and go, and he wished he could find a better home and work life balance.

Trying to control the sudden rage that was building in him he went and looked out of the window. What was he doing, working on a Sunday, two days before Christmas when he could have been with his wife and son? Palmer wondered how much longer he could remain in the force. He loved his job, and he was good at it, but he knew he was missing out with his family.

'Are you okay?' Elly appeared behind him and rested her hand on his shoulder.

'I'm fine,' he said shrugging her off, sniffing and getting a grip of himself. 'I've got something I need you to do.'

'Okay.'

'I need you to find anything you can on the suicide of a boy named Jack that happened in the late nineties. I don't have a last name, but it was possibly in ninety-eight. Come back to me when you have something.'

'Is this related to the case?' she asked putting her hands on her curvy hips.

'I think it might be.'

'I'll get onto that right now,' Elly said turning and walking back to her desk, her heels clapping on the floor as she went.

Palmer returned to his desk and sat looking at his notes. He could see a link forming. Fishing, scouts, Dennis, Jack. Somehow, he was sure it all came back to this. But where did Wendy and Eddie fit in to it? He could feel that all of the pieces of the puzzle were there: they just needed to be slotted into place.

Picking up his notepad he moved over to the incident board and examined the evidence. The pictures of the victims, scenes of the crimes, maps and the timeline – none of it yet added up. His eyes finally rested on the artist's impression of the suspect. There was something generic about the face yet strangely familiar, but he couldn't put his finger on what it was.

When his stomach rumbled, he knew it was time to take a break for lunch and decided it was the perfect opportunity to call home and speak to his son and wife. He needed to hear their voices and, more importantly, he needed them to know he was thinking about them and that he wished he was with them at home.

After consuming a serving of cottage pie and peas in the police station canteen, Palmer stepped outside the front of the building to call his family. To his bitter disappointment there was no answer. He remembered his wife was taking their son to visit Father Christmas. He wanted so badly to call and hear their voices, but he refrained from making the call. He'd have to speak to them later.

Looking up at the white sky he could feel that snow was in the air again. The chill had returned and the threat of rain was long gone. On the road in front of the station puddles were beginning to freeze over, a paper-thin layer of ice forming almost in front of his eyes. Rubbing his hands together for warmth he returned to the station and was met by Elly who was tearing down the stairs.

'I found it!' she said holding a printout in her hand. 'Jack Hucknell. He was a boy scout who killed himself in 1998. His parents found him at home. The newspaper doesn't give much information, but I've managed to track his family down. Here's the address.'

'Excellent.' Palmer took the papers from her.

'Poor little mite was thirteen.' She shook her head. 'Same age as my little sister. There's so much pressure on kids now. Social media, exams, it's so much for them to contend with. Doesn't bear thinking about.'

'No. It doesn't,' Palmer said thinking about his own son again. 'Fancy a trip.' He paused to look at the address. 'To Sawston?'

Palmer had called ahead and warned the Hucknell family that officers were on their way over to the house to interview them. He felt awful having to dredge up their painful past, especially with it being so close to Christmas but, in order to save another family pain, he had to subject this one to it. It was a dilemma he'd never got his head around properly.

Sawston, a large village south of Cambridge, was busy with shoppers. The high street was bustling with families doing some last-minute Christmas shopping. But it was a relief to be somewhere where the traffic flowed more freely than it did in the city. The Christmas lights came on just as darkness began to fall and the car pulled onto the high street.

'My son would have loved seeing that,' Palmer muttered to himself as he searched for The Dairy House through the window.

'Stop!' Elly exclaimed. 'It's just there.'

The grade-two listed terraced cottage was picture perfect. On the front door hung a large wreath. Through the window the warm glow from the lights flooded out onto the street. It was inviting. Like a Christmas card you might wish to step into.

'I always wanted to live in a house like this,' Elly said while getting out of the car and admiring the cottage.

'Nice place.' Palmer agreed locking the car. 'Let's not keep them too long, shall we? I'm sure they've got other things they'd rather be doing right now.'

'Yes.' Elly nodded remembering the reason they were there and knocked on the door.

'Hello?' A balding man opened the door.

'Mr Hucknell?'

'Yes that's right.'

'I'm DI Palmer and this is Sergeant Hale. We spoke to your wife a little while ago?'

'We've been expecting you,' he said beckoning for the officers to come in. 'It's getting chilly again.' He closed the door behind them. 'Won't you follow me.'

Palmer and Elly followed Mr Hucknell through the hall and into the large L-shaped sitting room. A fire was burning and the room had a gentle smell of wood and coal.

'Thank you for agreeing to talk to us,' Palmer said, while Elly admired the beautifully decorated tree which stood proud and tall in the corner of the room.

'My wife is just in the kitchen,' the man explained. 'Can I get you both a homemade mince pie?'

'Yes please,' Elly and Palmer both said in harmony.

'Wonderful. I'll just bring them through. Do take a seat.'

He pointed to the large red sofa covered in silky cushions and Palmer and Elly did as instructed. The sofa was placed opposite the fireplace and, while the pair waited for Mrs Hucknell and her husband to return, they found themselves getting lost watching the flames dance and lick around the charred logs.

'Here we go.'

A woman appeared carrying a tray with a plate of steaming mince pies on it. She placed it down on the coffee table in front of the sofa. Both Elly and Palmer sat up having relaxed and sunk into the cushions.

'That's very kind,' Palmer said salivating. 'We really appreciate you agreeing to talk to us.'

'I have to say,' the woman said turning to look at her husband, 'the call did come a bit out of the blue.'

'We understand it is a very difficult subject, but we think that a spate of recent murders might, somehow, be linked to your son's death.' Palmer refrained from picking up a mince pie yet. It didn't seem appropriate.

'You mean Dennis Wade?' the husband asked.

'Yes. There have been two further murders. Do the names Wendy Connor or Edward Kilpatrick mean anything to you?'

Both husband and wife shook their heads.

Mrs Hucknell said, 'We knew Dennis a little bit, of course. He was the scout leader for Jack's group. He seemed like a nice man, from the small amount of contact we had with him.'

'I hate to ask, but would you mind telling us a bit about your son's death?' Palmer had already seen the death certificate, so knew more than he was letting on, but wanted to hear what happened from their point of view.

'He'd been a happy boy,' Mr Hucknell said clenching his hands together. 'Jack was smart. He did well in school and he was popular.'

His wife reached out and rested her hand on his knee. The twenty years that had passed only helped to lessen the pain. They would never fully recover from losing their child.

'It all changed when he started secondary school,' Mrs Hucknell took over explaining. 'He suddenly became introverted. His schoolwork slipped, and he stopped being interested in things. He'd always loved his sport, was always out kicking a ball, but he even lost interest in that. We took him to the doctor. They said he was depressed but they didn't want to medicate him because of his age. We all hoped it was just a phase and that it would pass. But he started to have trouble sleeping and things got worse.' The pain in her voice was evident and Palmer couldn't help thinking about his own boy. 'He'd loved scouts and even lost his enthusiasm for that. We thought maybe it was hormones, a teenage thing.

'At the time his father worked for a bank and I worked as a doctor's receptionist. That day he went off to school as usual and the two of us went to work. The school was only a ten-minute walk from our house so we'd given Jack a key, so he could let himself into the house after school. He'd been doing it for months.' Her voice wavered. 'School finished at three twenty and I came back from work at five thirty.' Mrs Hucknell's bottom lip began to quiver and the officers could see she was doing her best to control it, which only made it harder to watch.

'His brother, Matthew, found him,' Mr Hucknell cut in, saving his wife the agony. 'Jack hung himself. Nina came home after work and found Matthew and Jack together. Matthew had come home later than Jack. He'd been playing tennis after school. He found Jack. He cut him down and sat on the floor next to his body until Nina came home and discovered them together.'

'I see,' Palmer said gravely.

'Matthew was never the same again. We sold the house, it held too many memories, and moved a few streets down. We've been here ever since. When Matthew was eighteen, he had a breakdown and was hospitalised. He lives on medication now.'

'Where is Matthew?' Elly asked.

'He moved away. We don't see him very often. He finds it hard being around us after what happened to his brother,' Nina said.

'He blamed us,' Mr Hucknell spat. 'As if we were to blame. We did everything we could. Yes, he lost his brother but we lost our son. We still don't have any answers. "Depression" the doctors said and that's it. Nothing else. Why was he depressed? He had a loving family, a nice home. It never made any sense.'

'He was hurting, Anthony, he didn't mean it.'

'It felt like we lost both our boys.' His eyes misted up.

'I know this is painful, but can you confirm what Jack used to kill himself with?'

'Rope. He must have got it out of the shed.' Nina's voice continued to quiver. 'I've got a picture of him if you'd like to see it?' It was clear she needed to replace the image in her head with something else.

'That would be lovely,' Elly said softly.

'I'll just go and fetch it.' Nina got up, her navy floral dress swishing as she went.

'My wife still finds it difficult,' Anthony said reaching for a mince pie. 'We've never had proper closure because we still don't know why he did it. I know that people who suffer from depression commit suicide but the change in him was so sudden, it just doesn't make any sense. We still don't have answers.' He wiped some loose pastry crumbs from his moustache. 'I suppose we never will.'

Palmer looked at Elly for a moment before deciding to speak.

'It is possible that these murders are somehow connected to what happened to Jack.' He was cautious not to say too much. 'Where does Matthew live?'

'Northampton.'

'Could I have his address please?' Palmer got out his trusty notebook. 'We'd like to speak to him.'

'Well, I wouldn't advise that.' Anthony glared at Palmer. 'He's very unstable.'

'I understand. We'll be very sensitive, but I think it is important that we do speak to him.'

'It might spark an episode,' Anthony said warily.

'If you'd like, you are very welcome to be present when we speak to him?'

'I'd be no use.' Anthony shook his head. 'But his mother might be. He's better with her than he is with me.'

'Here we are,' Nina said brightly coming back into the room just as Elly and Palmer both gave in and helped themselves to a mince pie each.

'This was taken in ninety-six. Look,' she said pointing at a figure, 'there's Dennis. This was one of their camping trips, I think. And here, in the middle, is Jack.' Nina handed the photo over to Palmer who studied it for a moment.

It was a picture of a scout group outside. Palmer looked at Jack. He was a slip of a boy, blonde, gangly but smiling. The other boys were smiling and looking happy too. On the right of the gang stood Dennis looking proudly at the camera. To his left stood a young woman. She was younger than Dennis but older than the boys. She must have been about eighteen. Palmer pointed her out to Elly without saying a word. It was Wendy. There was no doubt about it. She was younger, but her face hadn't changed much.

On the other side of the group stood another man, also smiling at the camera. It was Eddie Kilpatrick.

Palmer and Elly looked at each other and put down their half-eaten mince pies.

'May we borrow this for a while?' Palmer asked.

'Why?' Nina looked uncomfortable.

'Just for our records,' Palmer answered quickly. 'We'd like to make a copy of the picture. I can assure you we will return the original to you shortly.'

'Well, I suppose so.' Nina still wasn't convinced. 'But you must bring it back. It's the last picture I have of Jack looking happy.'

Chapter 26

'Morning, everyone.' Barrett stood in front of his team. 'Yesterday evening, Joe spoke to Mr and Mrs Hucknell, the parents of a boy called Jack who committed suicide in 1998. The boy was a member of the scout group that Dennis Wade led. The family have given us this photograph.' Barrett pointed to a blown-up version of the picture on a large white screen. 'You can see here that both Wendy Matlock, then Connor, and Eddie Kilpatrick appear in this photograph. We were working on the assumption that the killings were linked somehow to the golf club but now we want our focus to turn to the scout group.

'It's been confirmed that Dennis Wade and Eddie Kilpatrick stopped communicating sometime soon after the boy's suicide. Jack's parents both have alibis for each murder, which check out, but we are keen to speak to Matthew Hucknell, Jack's brother. He's been in and out of psychiatric units for the last twenty years and is more or less estranged from his family, who he blames for his brother's death. We have his address and officers have visited the premises but there is no sign of Matthew. Our priority now is to find Matthew Hucknell. We will be working closely with Northamptonshire police who have issued a search for the suspect. I want you all to dig into Matthew's life. Find out what you can and report to me. Clear?'

Mumblings of 'yes, sir' travelled around the room as the team dispersed and returned to their desks.

Palmer, who had a strange expression on his face, slowly made his way up to the white board.

'What is it, Joe?' Barrett asked examining his colleague's odd gaze.

'I know that face.' He pointed to a brown-haired lad who stood between two other scouts. 'It's him. I wasn't paying attention to the other boys' faces but now it's been enlarged I know it's him. He's been right under our noses the entire time.'

'Get your coat. We're going to pay the Hucknells another visit. We need to know exactly what we're dealing with.'

***

Tilly met Steven at twelve thirty at the bar of The Fort St George pub as they had agreed. He looked handsome in his jeans and green jumper, with his hair pushed back off his forehead. When she walked in out of the cold, he was already waiting for her and had ordered her a drink.

'Thank you.' She accepted the gin and tonic and clinked glasses with his pint of ale.

'Let's grab a seat and order,' Steven said looking around the heaving pub. 'I'm starving.'

'It's very busy,' Tilly commented, thinking they'd be lucky if they found an available table.

'Two for lunch.' Steven lent over the bar and smiled at the waitress.

'You'll be lucky.' The buxom woman laughed. 'We've been fully booked for weeks. You do know it's Christmas Eve?' she said, her eyes smiling.

'Yes, I'm aware of that.' Steven brandished a gleaming grin. 'Looks like we'll just have to get drunk,' he said turning to Tilly.

'You are naughty.' She sipped her drink and realised she'd not been in a room with so many people since before the murders began. A creeping sense of dread started to return. 'But seriously, I'm hungry. Shall we try somewhere else when we've finished these?' She held up her glass.

'Can do,' Steven said wiping the froth from his beer off his top lip. 'Where do you fancy?'

For a moment, Tilly thought he'd said *who* do you fancy, and she felt herself blushing.

'I don't mind. Anywhere that has a table and food.' She tripped over the words, her nerves starting to bother her again.

'What about my place?'

She looked at him with doubt.

'I can cook.' He laughed. 'I've not made it this far without being able to rustle up a tasty plate or two.'

'Okay then,' she agreed feeling like their meeting had just taken a more intimate turn.

'Great. We can stop by the shop and pick something up on the way there.'

'Where do you live?'

'Trafalgar Road. It's just the other side of the river. A couple minutes' walk. Not far. What do you want to eat?'

'I'm not fussy. I'll eat anything.' She paused to think for a moment. 'Just maybe not Chinese. My flatmate is Chinese and it's all she cooks. I love it, but I've had enough Chinese food over the last few days to last me a lifetime.'

'Lucky for you I'm more of a steak and chips kinda guy.'

'Suits me.' Tilly smiled, playing with the cuff on her jumper and noticing a small hole, which she couldn't help fiddling with.

'How you doing anyway? You seemed a bit freaked out last time I saw you.'

'You noticed.' Her voice was mousy.

'I think we all did.' He scratched the back of his neck, not wanting to make her feel bad but deciding it was best to be honest. 'How come you were so upset about Dennis's glasses?'

'I don't know. I guess, seeing him like that, in the shop, when I found him, it just wasn't right. He didn't look like Dennis. In my head, if I could fix how he looked then maybe it wouldn't be so bad. I know that sounds nuts.' She looked at the floor.

'Not really. I understand wanting to fix something. It's normal. Don't worry about it.'

Steven rubbed her upper arm with his hand gently. He had a way of making her feel relaxed and she liked it.

'Thanks. I really felt so silly.' She stumbled over the words apologetically.

'It can't have been nice for you finding him. I'm sorry.' He finished his beer and banged the glass down on the bar to emphasis it. 'Let's get out of here, shall we?' He offered her his arm and she linked hers through it.

'Let's go.' Tilly smiled unhooking her bag off the back of the bar stool before being led out of the pub and onto the wintery landscape of Midsummer Common just as small flakes began to drift down from the thick white sky.

'It's so pretty,' she said holding out a hand to catch a snowflake, which melted as soon as it made contact with her skin.

'Pretty but cold,' Steven said zipping his coat up. 'Not like Christmas in Sydney that's for sure.'

'Do you miss it?' Tilly asked as they walked side by side with their arms still linked.

'Sometimes.' He thought about it. 'Actually, a lot of the time. I'll be heading back there when all this is over.'

'When all what is over?' Tilly felt her heart sink. She'd miss him if he left.

'Christmas and stuff.' He walked with his gaze fixed on the path in front. 'Now that my mum has gone, there's not much left for me.'

'Why did you come back?' Tilly wondered if she was prying too much. 'If you don't mind me asking.'

'I had to deal with her death. The paperwork, the house, her funeral. It was only ever the two of us.'

'What about your dad?'

'Never knew him. Mum was young when she had me. He was older, married apparently. He wanted nothing to do with me.'

'That must have been tough.' Tilly moved closer to him as they carried on walking.

'Not really. You don't miss what you've never had.'

Fifteen minutes later, and after a quick stop-off at the local shop, they arrived at Steven's house just as the snow was falling thicker and faster.

Shaking her hair free from flakes Tilly felt an instant wave of heat as Steven opened the door to his home.

'That's better.' He pulled the door closed with a thud, put the bag of food down on the floor, unzipped his coat and slipped out of it before helping Tilly remove hers.

'Looks like we are going to have a white Christmas.' Tilly looked around the small living room. 'I think it's the first one in my lifetime.'

'How come you're still in Cambridge?' Steven asked, picking up the bag and making his way through to the kitchen.

'I can't explain it, but I just know if I leave now, I'll never come back.' She looked at a photo that stood on the sideboard. It was a picture of Steven and an older woman who she presumed was his mother.

'Nothing wrong with leaving the past where it belongs, if that's what you need to do.' He removed the packet of steak from the bag and threw it onto the counter.

'Don't you have plans tomorrow?' Tilly asked joining him in the kitchen.

'I think I'll start packing up mum's things.' He took a knife from the block and ran it through the plastic packaging.

'What will you do with this place?'

'Put it on the market. An agent can deal with the sale. I don't need to be here. I'd rather be on a beach in the sunshine.' He smiled at her before removing a heavy griddle pan from a cupboard. 'Why are you so interested?'

'Just curious, that's all,' Tilly said taking a seat at the small bistro table that was near the back door.

'Here.' He handed her a bottle of Rioja. 'Get that down you.'

'I'll be drunk as a skunk!' She laughed.

'I don't mean the whole bottle.' Steven handed over two glasses and a bottle opener. 'Pour us both a glass.'

Tilly did as instructed and handed one to her host.

'Oven chips okay?' he asked while removing a bag from the freezer.

'Absolutely.' Tilly found she had a proper appetite for the first time in weeks and she looked forward to enjoying the fruity red wine with the red meat. 'Thanks for offering to do this. It's really nice of you.'

'Not a problem.' Steven had his back to her as he poured some frozen chips onto a baking tray.

'Where's the loo?' The gin and tonic had gone right through her.

'Just through there,' he said pointing to a wooden sliding door on the left-hand side of the room. 'It's tiny, I warn you. This place must have been built when we were still a nation of midgets.'

Tilly slid the door back revealing what was essentially a cupboard with a toilet and miniature basin inside. She had to sit down on the bowl before she was able to close the door again. On her left were the tiny basin and a small mirror and on her right were two coat hooks, one of which was occupied. Sitting on the loo she looked up at the coat hanging there. It was a dark grey duffle coat with a hood. For a moment, while she looked at it, she wasn't sure what she was seeing. It looked like any man's coat but when she realised it was familiar the horror sank in. Tilly had seen the news. She'd seen the E-fit of the suspect and the picture of the coat the suspect was wearing. She knew then that she was looking at that exact coat.

Suddenly unable to pee, Tilly froze and claustrophobia set in. She was trapped with no way out except to go back through the kitchen. For a few moments she remained there, trying to prevent a panic attack, trying to work out how she could get away and trying to process how she'd ended up there.

Eventually, after three more minutes, she stood up, buttoned up her jeans and with a shaking hand pushed the sliding door back.

'Everything okay?' Steven asked over his shoulder holding a large kitchen knife in his right hand.

'I… erm… I…' She could feel the panic rising in her throat. 'I don't feel very well.' Tilly walked around the edge of the room putting as much distance between herself and him as possible. Steven was blocking her escape route.

'What's the matter?' He turned slowly, still grasping the knife. 'You look very pale.' He recognised the fear in her eyes. He'd seen that same look on the face of Dennis, Wendy and Eddie just before he'd killed them.

Unable to speak Tilly looked over at the loo and, in that moment, Steven knew she'd recognised the coat. He couldn't believe he'd been so careless.

'Sit down, Tilly.' He sighed pointing at one of the bistro chairs with the sharp end of the knife. 'You and I need to have a little talk.'

'I don't feel well.' She stuttered, 'I-I-I think I need to g-go home.'

'We've opened the wine now. At least finish your glass.' He took a step towards her. 'It would be bad manners to leave now.'

Never taking her eyes off the blade, which glinted in the daylight that poured through the glass in the back door, she did as she was told. With a quivering hand she picked up the wine glass and took a sip. The red, which had tasted sweet like jam, now tasted bitter.

'You're shaking.' Steven stood over Tilly still brandishing the knife. 'It's only a coat.' His eyes danced.

'Why?' Her throat was dry.

'Because I had to and because they deserved it.' He smiled and shrugged as if he were a schoolboy explaining away a cheap prank.

'Dennis had a family. He was a nice man and—'

'You know nothing!' Steven roared, grabbing Tilly by the throat and lifting her out of her chair. 'You don't know what he did.' He sprayed her with saliva as he spoke, and she thought she might be sick.

Before Tilly had time to react the front door of the house was smashed down and officers came flooding into the house shouting at Steven to let her go. For a second, she was certain he was going to shove the knife into her stomach. His eyes were burning with rage but a moment later he released her and was smiling like he was stoned.

'See you, Tilly,' he called over his shoulder while officers dragged him out of the house as Barrett read him his rights.

Palmer rushed over to Tilly who had collapsed back onto the bistro chair, unable to stand or support her own weight.

'You're safe now.' He put an arm around her shoulder. 'It's all over.'

Chapter 27

4.50pm Monday 24th December

'Interview commencing at 4.50pm on Monday the twenty-fourth of December. Officers present, DCI Barrett and DI Palmer,' Barrett said for the tape and for the record.

'Mr Steven Fisher, otherwise known as Mr Robert Mirren, has refused legal representation.'

'No one calls me Robert.' He smirked.

'What should we call you then?' Palmer asked.

'Robbie is fine.'

'Okay, Robbie it is then. So, Robbie, do you understand that you are under arrest for the murders of Dennis Wade, Wendy Matlock and Eddie Kilpatrick?'

'Sure.' He shrugged.

'This is your opportunity to tell us in your own words what happened,' Barrett said calmly. He could feel he was in the presence of someone damaged and dangerous and it was his job to try and get a confession.

'You think you know.' Robbie's eyes danced around the room. 'But you don't have the first clue.'

'So, tell us,' Palmer urged. 'Tell us about Jack Hucknell.'

Both inspectors watched as the suspect twitched when hearing the name.

'Jack.' He looked from one officer to another. 'Jack was my best friend. We did everything together. We were like brothers. I even joined the scouts so that we could spend time together.' Robbie shifted in his seat.

'Go on,' Barrett said evenly.

'We were kids. We just wanted to ride our bikes and muck about.' He started to look uncomfortable in his own skin. 'We just wanted to have fun like boys do. We told each other everything. The girls we fancied and stuff. We were really close. I didn't have any siblings. He was it.'

'Tell us about this,' Barrett said, sliding a photograph in a clear plastic evidence bag across the table to the suspect.

Robbie picked it up and held it close to his face, losing himself in the image.

'We were happy then. Look, Jack's smiling. You see?' He turned the photo around for the inspectors to see. 'I didn't know what was going to happen. It was meant to be an adventure.' Robbie's pitch grew more frantic. 'We were going camping. It was exciting. Jack and I had been looking forward to it for weeks. We'd snuck some sweets into our backpacks and I'd even stolen a couple of cigarettes from my mum. We were going to smoke them that night to see what it was like.'

Palmer remembered the first time he'd tried a cigarette. It had been enough to put him off smoking for life.

'We all met outside the social club that Saturday afternoon. It was surprisingly warm for October. Mum had taken me shopping to buy waterproofs especially for the trip.'

Barrett noticed the sad expression that crossed Robbie's face when he mentioned his mother.

'I had my bag packed and I was all ready to go. I'd only joined the scouts in September because Jack had done it for a while and kept telling me how great it was.' He stopped to consider something. 'Eddie shouldn't have been there. It wasn't meant to be him. The other scout leader was ill or something so Eddie was standing it. Mr Wade told us he didn't want to cancel the trip, but they needed another grown-up to come along. He introduced us to Eddie. We didn't pay much attention to him at first.' He bit his fingernails.

'What about Wendy?' Palmer asked.

'She was there,' Robbie hissed. 'She'd joined as a young scout leader. She often helped out.' The venom in his voice took Palmer by surprise.

'What happened?' Barrett wanted answers.

'We all got in the minibus and they took us to Burwell Lakes. There must have been fourteen boys in the group.

'When we got to the lakes we went fishing for a few hours. I remember thinking it was actually quite boring, but it beat being stuck at home doing nothing while Mum was at work.

'Later we walked across some fields to the edge of these woods. Dennis told us that we'd reached the spot and we needed to erect our tents. Dennis, Eddie and Wendy all had a tent each but us boys were split into pairs. I shared with Jack.

'After we'd all put our tents up, we had to cook our own dinner. We'd brought little stoves in our bags. We were going to get badges if we managed it. Jack and I had decided we were going to have baked beans and bacon and we cooked it by ourselves. We felt proud and grown-up.

'By then it was dark, and Dennis and Wendy had built a campfire. We were all told to come and sit round it in a circle. They made us sing songs. Stupid baby songs like *Row Row The Boat* and *Once I Caught A Fish Alive.*' There was a glint in his eye. Barrett and Palmer looked at each other.

'Then what happened?'

'Gradually the other boys got tired and went into their tents to sleep. But Jack and I were determined to stay up as late as possible. We were sat on one side of the fire and Eddie and Dennis were on the other side. I remember they had a hip flask they kept handing back and forth and topping up with a glass bottle of something.

'Jack and I were hoping we'd have a chance to sneak off and try the cigarette, but the grown-ups just wouldn't go to sleep. Eventually Wendy said goodnight and crawled into her tent but not Dennis or Eddie. Oh no, they were happy to stay up drinking.

'It must have been at about one in the morning. Jack and I were tired, but we had made this promise that we'd stay up later than anyone else and I suppose neither of us wanted to lose face by giving in first.

'I remember the fire was beginning to burn out. The flames had died down and all that remained were some glowing embers. Dennis and Eddie both got up at the same time. They were a bit shaky on their feet.

'Anyway, they said we should go with them into the woods to collect more fuel for the fire. Jack and I thought it was exciting. They had their torches and they led the way. We followed. I was actually a bit frightened. I could hardly see where I was going but I kept following the light. We both did.

'When we got into the woods Dennis said he'd take Jack and they'd search one area and I was told to go with Eddie and search the other way.' He stopped talking, not wanting to remember. 'You know what happened next,' Robbie said finally.

Barrett cleared his throat and put his hands on the table. 'I can hazard a guess, but we need to hear it on the record.'

'That night we went into those woods two innocent boys. When we came out again we were not the same.' His eyes fell to the floor. 'They did horrible, unspeakable things to us.'

'We need you to say it.' Palmer wished he didn't have to press the matter.

'They raped us,' Robbie said and looked up with a dead expression. 'They took us into the woods and they raped us.'

Barrett nodded slowly. There it was. The motive.

'Jack and I both knew what happened to one another, but we tried not to speak about it again. He never recovered.

'We kept going to scouts, and most of the time it was difficult for Dennis to get Jack on his own, but he managed it. I never saw Eddie again. It only ever happened to me once. But Jack, for him it carried on. After a while my mum let me leave the scouts. I never told her what had happened to Jack or me.

'Jack was so broken he even lost the ability to fight it. He went to scouts week-in and week-out without saying a word. Then, one day two years after it began, when he couldn't take it any more, he killed himself.' Robbie put his hands up around his own neck. 'He hung himself until his last breath left his body and he was finally free from that monster.'

The inspectors sat in silence. What was there to say? The law said an eye for an eye was wrong, but for a moment both men imagined themselves as young boys. They pictured the fear and pain Robbie and Jack had been subjected too and, for a split second, they could identify with the killer.

'Why Wendy?' Palmer asked suddenly, wanting to understand what she'd been punished for. 'Why did you have to kill her?'

'She saw us,' Robbie said. 'That night when they walked us back to the tents, she was awake. She saw us. I looked at her. She could see we'd been crying, and she watched through a gap in her tent as our abusers tucked us into our sleeping bags. She knew, and she never said a word.' A long silence prevailed.

'Why now? Why wait until now?' Barrett asked finally.

'I'd left. I'd got away from it all. It was in the past, but then my mum died and I had to come home. It was all here waiting for me when I got back, and I knew the only way to lay Jack's ghost to rest was to do this. He's been with me. He's always been with me, following me from country to country. He speaks to me and haunts my dreams.' Robbie looked distant, unhinged. 'I had to put it right. They had to pay for what they did to us.

'I knew Dennis wouldn't remember me. Jack was his special boy. I came up with fake name and got a part-time job in the shop. The rest was simple.' He looked down at the palms of his hands. 'Jack can rest now, can't you Jack.' He turned, smiling, and spoke into the thin air.

Chapter 28

He stood outside the front door holding a bag of presents. He was nervous. He'd not done this for a long time. He hoped he'd be able to enjoy himself.

Palmer opened the door and shook hands with his colleague. 'Ian, come in.' Barrett had never heard Palmer use his first name before.

'Here you are.' Barrett handed the presents over awkwardly. 'Just some things for your boy.'

'That's very kind. Thank you,' Palmer said taking Barrett's coat and hanging it on the coat stand. 'Lucas is very excited you're coming. He's been talking about it all morning,' Palmer said and led Barrett into the living room.

Lucas, his son, was sat on the floor playing with a train set he'd just unwrapped. 'Hello.' The small boy looked up at the tall policeman. He had his father's eyes.

'Hello.' Barrett knelt down. 'That's a nice train.'

'Do you want to play with me?' Lucas asked, his expression full of hope.

'Let Ian come and say hello to Mummy first,' Palmer said ruffling his son's hair.

'Okay,' the boy said and returned to pushing his train around the wood track.

'Sally,' Barrett said warmly as he entered the kitchen to find her setting the table with crackers.

A candelabra with red candles stood pride of place in the middle of the table and the white tablecloth was decorated with small gold stars. It was the kind of table his wife would have approved of.

'Good to see you, Ian.' She beamed planting a small kiss on his cheek. 'So pleased you could join us.'

'Time for the good stuff.' Palmer reached into the fridge and removed a bottle of champagne, brandishing it in the air.

'I'll get the glasses.' Sally removed her pinstripe apron and hung it on the back of the door.

'We got him,' Palmer said quietly so that his wife wouldn't hear. 'We got the sod.'

'He's going to be transferred to a psychiatric prison. He attempted suicide last night,' Barrett said gravely.

'How?' Palmer knew that the police were tasked with taking all precautions necessary to ensure prisoners in their care did not come to harm.

'He was smashing his head against a door. He kept doing it repeatedly. He split the skin on his skull and forehead but kept on going. They got him to hospital in time. He's very bruised and is now catatonic.'

'Wow. That's violent,' Palmer said raising his eyebrows.

'What are you two gossiping about?' Sally appeared holding three champagne flutes. 'I'll have no speak of work.'

'Wouldn't dream of it.' Palmer winked at Barrett.

'Good. Now pour me a drink. That beef isn't going to carve itself.'

'Please, Mum.' Lucas appeared in the doorway. 'Please can the policeman come and play trains?'

Sally turned to Barrett offering him the final decision.

'One quick game before lunch.' Barrett smiled and accepted a glass of fizz from Palmer. 'It is Christmas day after all.'

Epilogue

11.00am Thursday 3rd January

Barrett and Palmer arrived at Rampton Secure Hospital, a high-security psychiatric hospital, in time for their appointment with Doctor Giles Megaw, the chief psychiatrist at the unit.

The drive from Cambridge to north Nottinghamshire had been longer than they'd expected. The snow had long since melted and the ground was now hard with frost as the inspectors got out of their car and made their way to the front entrance of the imposing building.

After showing their badges to the guards the men were led down a long corridor before being shown into an office at the end.

'Doctor Megaw.' Barrett shook hands with the short man who wore a blue shirt with navy trousers.

'Have a seat, gentlemen.' He pointed to two leather chairs on the other side of his desk before sitting back down in his own seat.

'How's the patient?' Palmer asked.

Megaw considered this for a moment before answering. 'Not fit to stand trial if that's what you're asking.' He looked over his reading glasses at them.

'We wanted to talk to you because there has been a development.' Barrett sat back in his chair and crossed one leg over the other. 'It has a bearing on your patient.'

'Oh?' The doctor rested his chin on his hand and waited patiently.

'It seems that Mr Mirren was related to one of his victims. Edward Kilpatrick was Robert Mirren's biological father.'

'How can that be?' The doctor, who was flustered by the news, began sorting through the file he had on Robbie, which lay in front of him on his desk. 'Robbie did not know his father.'

'The DNA matches. Edward was his father. Now, we don't know any of the details because Robert's mother is dead, but DNA has confirmed it to be true. And we have Edward's diaries that mention a GM. Robert's mother was Georgia Mirren.'

The psychiatrist sat back in his seat absorbing the information.

'Edward Kilpatrick sexually abused my patient,' he said steadily.

'Yes, we know.' Barrett confirmed uncrossing his legs and leaning forward. 'We don't believe Edward Kilpatrick had any knowledge that Robbie was his son. He wasn't even usually involved in the scouts. It was a case of him being in the wrong place at the wrong time. We've spoken to Mrs Kilpatrick—'

'That must have been an awkward conversation,' the doctor blurted out, interrupting.

'And,' Barrett continued, 'neither she nor Eddie had any knowledge of Robbie's existence. She's told us that in 1983 and four she knew her husband was having an affair. Apparently, she confronted her husband and said she would leave and take their small daughter with her unless he put an end to it. As far as Susan Kilpatrick is concerned that was the end of it. The dates do tie in and the DNA confirms it.'

'Robbie grew up thinking his father abandoned him,' Megaw said thoughtfully. 'In fact, you are telling me that he didn't know he existed.'

'That's about the sum of it, doctor,' Palmer said.

'This is a troubling development.' Megaw scrunched his eyes up. 'Do we know if Kilpatrick abused anyone else. His daughter perhaps?'

'We've spoken to Marie Kilpatrick who denies her father ever laid a hand on her. I believe her, personally,' Palmer said.

'Abusers do tend to have a type. It's uncommon for a paedophile to like boys and girls,' the doctor informed them.

'We are certain that Eddie did not know Robbie was his son.'

'Well that's something, I suppose.' He paused. 'I think knowledge of any of this could tip him right over the edge. My patient is unstable enough already. That revelation could be the final straw.'

'Which is why we wanted to talk to you directly,' Barrett cut in.

'What would you like me to do, gentlemen?' The doctor held his hands up.

'You are his psychiatrist. We thought it might be better if it came from you.'

'Does he really need to know?' Megaw asked.

'He has a half-sister,' Palmer explained.

'And this sister wants a relationship with him?' The doctor did nothing to hide his scepticism.

'No, she doesn't. But she may come looking for answers one day.'

Doctor Megaw stood up and faced both men. 'Gentlemen, I would request that you'd accompany me for a moment. There is something I think you should see.'

Palmer and Barrett looked at one another before getting up and following Megaw back along the corridor and up some stairs.

'This is where we keep patients who have to be separated from the rest of the population.' Megaw stumped up the stairs. 'Robbie is being kept in isolation. He will be very groggy from the medication.'

'Why did you separate him?' Palmer asked as they continued to climb another level.

'He became uncontrollably aggressive. He is a danger to the staff, other patients and himself.'

'What sparked it off?' Barrett wanted to know.

'He is delusional, Detective. He believes his childhood friend is talking to him. He was sure that by killing those three people he would be released from his torment, but the voices still exist. We are treating him for severe schizophrenia but there may also be an underlying personality disorder,' the doctor explained as they arrived on D Wing. 'I want you to see exactly what we are dealing with here,' he said as he led them to a door with a small window in it. 'Look through there.'

Barrett peered through the safety glass. In the far corner of the room sat Robbie huddled in a ball. He was talking to someone who wasn't there.

'You see?' Doctor Megaw said. 'To you he is a criminal, but to me he is a victim and a patient.'

'You're a good man, Doctor.' Barrett nodded.

'I do my job and I don't let myself get emotionally involved.' He looked coy. 'I'm not here to judge.'

'Will you tell him about his father?' Palmer asked.

'Perhaps in time.' Megaw sighed. 'Right now, our priority is stabilising him.'

At that moment they heard a crash come from the other side of the door. Standing on his tiptoes, the doctor looked through the small window. Slowly Robbie's bruised face appeared in the glass as if from nowhere. He was looking right through the doctor as if they were invisible when, out of the blue, he started banging his head on the door.

'One, two, three, four, five.' Each thud of his head on the glass was in time to the rhythm. 'Once I caught a fish alive.'

Bang. Bang.

'Six, seven, eight, nine, ten.'

Bang. Bang.

'Then I let him go again.'

Bang. Bang.

'Why did you let him go?'

Bang.

'Because he bit my finger so.'

Bang. '

Which finger did he bite?'

Bang.

'This little finger on the right…'

THE END

Acknowledgements

Let me start by saying that, as always, I have a number of wonderful people to thank. My editor, Clare Law, who always helps to bring out the best in my work. The proofreader who has the hideous task of tidying up my dyslexic typos. The wonderful team at Bloodhound Books who read, advise, polish, format and market my work. You are the best. The readers who take a punt on me and pick up my work. The wonderful people in my ARC group. My fabulous beta readers. The lovely people who bother to take the time to review my books. My family and friends who support me and put up with all my foibles. Without all of you, my dream of being a writer would have remained simply that.

Thank you xx

Author's Note

I have spent fourteen years of my life building a career as a writer and, in more recent times, a publisher. On the whole, the industry is a supportive place but as with most things in life, there are exceptions. Perhaps due to the fact that I don't apologise for my ambition and given the fact that I proud to be able to make a living out of a career I love, I have alienated a few people along the way, but I will continue to provide for my family and I will never apologise for that. In fact, I thank those who have been negative because they have only helped to make me stronger, wiser and more resolute.

Sometimes the greatest way to say something is to say nothing… but I'm a writer and words are my sword.